BROTHERS IN ARMS

FAMILY BY CHOICE

BLOOD RELATIONS
BROTHERS IN ARMS

PRAISE FOR BLOOD RELATIONS

"[Blood Relations] is an action packed adventure that will appeal to fans of fantasy, vampire stories and science fiction. (...) I suspect there will be many [fans of the series]."

Alejandro Bustos, Apartment 613,

http://apt613.ca

"I took *Blood Relations* with me on my latest trip to read when I found time. I have taken books with me on trips before, but I never seem to find time to read them. I not only found time to read this one, but I finished it as well. It's wonderfully written. Alex is a character who is very real and the reader can understand his background and his motives, whether you agree with them or not. This is a story with more layers than you would expect from yet another "vampire story".

If you like a hard, gritty story and/or a supernatural tale with a lot of reality thrown in, you will enjoy *Blood Relations*."

Geeky Godmother reviews,

http://geekygodmother.ca

BROTHERS IN ARMS

BY CAROLINE FRECHETTE

BOOK 2 OF THE FAMILY BY CHOICE SERIES

Renaissance

Cover art by Franck Formantin.
Cover design by Caroline Fréchette.
Interior design by Natasha Brousseau.

Legal deposit, Library and Archives Canada, March 2014.
ISBN 978-0-9920420-8-0
1. Winters, Alex (fictitious character) – Fiction. 2. Superpowers – Fiction. 3. Mafia – Fiction. I. Title.
Renaissance Press
http://renaissancebookpress.com
info@renaissancebookpress.com

For Cédric and Maxime.

You guys were my first superheroes.

I take another sip of my coffee and check the time on my cell phone. The jackass is late. Again. I had my doubts when I put him in charge, and every chance I get, I see that I should have listened to my first instincts. Too bad I didn't really have anyone better to do the job. I've had enough, this time, though. I don't put down the phone, but dial Jimmy's number. It takes him a couple rings to answer, and I tell him to come pick me up. If Chris hasn't shown up by the time Jimmy gets here, I'm coming down to his place and kicking the crap out of him. I'm not sure I won't do that anyway, to tell the truth. I blow out the smoke and put out my cigarette in the aluminum ashtray before signaling the waitress for more coffee. The little old lady sitting at the table across from me gives me a dirty look, piles some change on the table and gets up to walk away. Good. She was bothering me anyway. They're talking about passing a law in this town against smoking even outside. I know I smoke a lot, but I ain't gonna fill up the entire atmosphere with my smoke, and if anyone could, one city's smoke ban isn't gonna do dick to stop it.

My coffee's just arrived when Chris shows up. The bastard doesn't even have the decency to look ashamed

1

of himself. He's grinning, and his step has kind of a swagger in it, like he's proud. He turns the chair around to lean his arms on the back as he sits in front of me. I pull up my sleeve and look at my wrist in an exaggerated gesture, even though I'm not wearing a watch, to let him know how I feel about his tardiness. He doesn't seem to notice, just grins at me.

"Hey boss!"

I sigh, and take a sip of my coffee.

"You're late."

He rolls his eyes, still smiling, and waves his hand dismissively.

"It's only like, twenty minutes or so."

I take out another smoke and make fire between my fingers, holding it there for a good ten seconds before I light my cigarette with it, then stay quiet and glare at him for a few moments. He doesn't seem to take the hint. I guess when everyone in your organization already knows you have super-powers, it's not that impressive anymore. I vanish the fire and breathe out the smoke.

"It's half an hour. And I don't appreciate being kept waiting. I've mentioned this already."

He shrugs, and starts to look inside his coat. I'm so pissed, it's hard to contain the fire; the coffee in the mug I'm holding starts to boil. Again, he doesn't notice, and I take a closer look. His eyes are half-lidded and bloodshot, and his pupils are huge. His movements are sluggish and uncoordinated. I try not to hiss, but I talk through my teeth.

"Are you high?"

He shrugs one shoulder, looking halfway between amused and guilty, the kind of guilt you have when you're caught eating cookies before dinner.

"So what if I am?"

I breathe through my nose. The fire's been hard to keep down lately, and with this issue being so close to home, it's hard not to burn him alive right now. But he's just an idiot, and it's not his fault. Well, not totally anyway, though I'm sure the drugs didn't help.

"You know the rules. You do not get high before coming to see me. I shouldn't have to be telling you this."

He raises his hands, showing me the palms.

"Hey, relax, man! You can be such a tight-ass!"

I throw away the cigarette, reach over and grab him by the shirt, twisting the cloth and pulling him down, my hand right under his chin, so that the collar is wrapped tight around his throat. He gasps, and his eyes go wide. I put my face close to his, close enough to smell the weed on him. I keep my voice low. I don't want to make a scene, here, and it's not the volume that counts, but the tone. Besides, from his expression, I can see I'm making the right impression on him.

"You listen close, asshole. We are not friends, you and me. I could never be friends with the likes of you. You have a job to do, and you report to me, that's all there is to it. If you don't take that seriously, if you don't show the proper respect, or if you show up late or high one more time, you and me are gonna have a problem. Got it?"

He nods, and I let go of his shirt. I pick up my coffee and blow on it, deliberately. He's breathing hard, and I can tell that he's wondering what to do.

"Now hand over the money and get out of here. You make me sick."

He grabs the envelope out of his jacket, dumps it on the table and scrambles away. Some people give us glances, but I don't care. This place isn't one of my usual hangouts, so all I have to do is not come back. I pick up the envelope and take a look inside. I'm not sure exactly, but there seems to be less money than there should be. I don't have the leisure to count it right now, so I try taking a sip of my coffee, but it's too hot. It doesn't burn; I'm pretty much immune to all sorts of heat, but it doesn't taste like much when it's this hot.

I take out another cigarette and sigh, rubbing my face in my left hand. It's been a long day. It's about time it was over. I see movement at the corner of my eye, and I turn, expecting Jimmy, but it's some weird-looking guy I've never seen before. He's wearing a hundred-buck cheap ready-made suit, sunglasses, and has his hair slicked out on the side with way too much gel. He stops at my table and smiles at me. I take a sip from my coffee, trying to ignore him. He doesn't go away, though, and even has the affront to flip the chair that Chris was sitting on so he can have a seat at my table. I look pointedly at the dozen or so empty tables on the terrace, and then back at him, eyebrow raised. It doesn't faze him. What is it with people testing my limits today? Did I wake up in Testosterone City?

"Can I help you?"

"Alex Winters?"

I frown, and take a closer look. This guy doesn't look like a cop, or a lawyer, or even a wise guy. What could he possibly want with me?

"What do you want?"

He reaches inside his jacket, and I scramble to make my thoughts ready to burn him alive before he shoots me, but he only pulls out a business card. I take it. Who knows? Whatever it is he has to say might be interesting. It's printed with blue raised ink, and has a weird medical-like logo on the right. The left side simply says *GenEx Group* and has a phone number under that.

"I'll take that as a yes. My name is Donald Finley, and I represent the GenEx Group. Have you heard of us?"

"Never."

I put the card down and resume drinking my coffee, trying to look as uninterested as I can, which is actually hard because I'm kind of curious now.

"We are a corporation that works with people of your... particular abilities."

I raise an eyebrow. That could mean many things, when it comes to me. But when people are this vague about it, it usually means my ability to manipulate fire with my mind. He's got my attention now. I've never met anyone else that could do the things I can. Maybe this guy has. Then again, maybe not.

"So?"

"So, as you may suspect, people like you are few and far between. Our purpose is to help them."

The only way this guy has heard of me is through what I do; he should know better than most how well I've done for myself in the past few years.

"I don't need any help."

The waitress starts to come over, but I wave her away. I don't want others overhearing this conversation.

"Fair enough. However, we could help each other."

I light another cigarette, this time using my lighter. There's no need to show off now, and I'm starting to think maybe I should put a lid on it, if people like this guy are seeking me out in cafés I don't usually go to.

"Keep talking."

"Our facilities are dedicated to try and understand what makes you so... unique, but also how such miracles can be physically possible."

Try and understand? That doesn't sound like anything I want to have any part of.

"That sounds like research."

"Well, yes, part of our *raison d'être* is research."

"No way. I'm not anybody's guinea pig."

"You misunderstand me. Through our research, you would gain better control of your abilities. You would be able to accomplish things you never even thought to try before. None of our experiments are harmful, or even unpleasant. And in return for your help, we could provide you with opportunities better suited to your... talents."

I take a moment to consider him, watching him carefully. He looks like a snake. There is no way I'm trusting this guy, he's got the stink of dishonesty all over him.

"I've got plenty of opportunities right here. If you heard of what I do, you heard I'm good at it."

"I'm sure you are. But this would require far less of your time, and we could pay you handsomely."

"I'm already paid handsomely. I'm not interested."

"We could match any price you throw at us."

I frown at him. He has to know I'm a man of means; and judging by how cheap his suit is, he probably isn't. The fact that he's willing to pay anything arouses my suspicion. He's way too desperate; this has a catch so big I'm surprised I don't already see it.

"I said I'm not interested. Now get out of here."

"Is there nothing I can say to change your mind?"

"Do I need to spell it out for you? Aren't you science types good with words? Not. Interested. Scram."

He shakes his head slightly, sighing, but stands up.

"I'm very sorry we couldn't come to an agreement. Have a good day. Until we meet again, Mister Winters."

I finish my cigarette, watching him go, making sure he's walking away, and I get another one out of my case, bringing it to my lips. Just as I'm about to light it, I see Jimmy coming to join me on the terrace, and I get up, leaving a twenty on the table instead of lighting the smoke. He joins me, and looks like he was about to settle down, but when he sees me leave, he just shrugs and follows. I hand him a cigarette, 'cause I know he's about to ask for one, and I light up as we walk toward the car. I'm about to walk around to the passenger's side, but he throws me the keys, and I have to think fast to catch them. I try not to groan. I'm not in the mood for his driving lessons today.

"Again?"

He shrugs, taking out his Zippo to light his smoke, going toward the passenger's side.

"Yeah, again. How you gonna learn if you don't ever do it?"

I sigh. He's right, and I did promise him I'd learn this year so he doesn't have to drive me around all the time. But I'm in a foul mood, and I know what that does to my skills.

"Fine. But it's your funeral."

He chuckles, letting out the smoke and sitting down in the car.

"Seeing as I should have had ten funerals already, I'm pretty confident."

"Whatever."

I start the car, and I stall the engine before I've even pulled into the street. I swear at it, and Jimmy laughs at me. I breathe through my nose as I start the engine again.

"Shut up, Jimmy. Why can't you get a nice automatic, anyway?"

"I do it all for you. If you don't learn standard, it's not worth learning how to drive at all."

"I don't care! I'm never gonna buy a standard car!"

He shrugs, and stays quiet as I pull into the street. I have to concentrate on everything I do. I've only been learning for a couple weeks, and so far, I hate it with a passion.

"So, how'd things go with Chris?"

"What? Oh. Usual, I guess. There's something I don't like about that guy."

"Yeah, he's kind of a dick."

"Half our guys are dicks. Him, though, it's something else. He showed up high today. And I didn't have time to count to make sure, but I think his payment wasn't all there."

"What did you do?"

"Well, I put him in his place about the drugs. But I couldn't look in the envelope until he was gone."

He stays quiet for a minute.

"So... I'm guessing you want me to look into it?"

"Yeah. Would you?"

"Sure."

I slow down for a stop sign, and even though I don't come to a complete stop, I still manage to stall the car. I curse at it, start it up again, and Jimmy laughs at me. It's a while before he starts talking again.

"So, I ran into Joe Tyler today."

I see another stop sign, and kind of just slow down before I go through. I'm going a little fast, but at least I don't stall this time. I'll pay the ticket if I get one, I don't care, as long as I don't have to start in first gear again.

"So?"

"So, he tells me you gave him another week for his payment."

I grit my teeth, and I press on the brake too hard at the red light, stalling the stupid car again. The key clicks in the ignition three times before I realize I'm not pressing down on the clutch.

"So what? It's my decision."

"Well, you can't just do that. That guy's been late for three weeks, now. You've gotta do something about it. Set an example."

"Why don't you do it yourself? It is kind of your job."

"Well I can't very well do my job when my boss keeps giving him extensions, can I?"

I press too hard on the gas pedal, and the car jumps forward. I try to calm down. Whatever I think about paying tickets, it's not like I actually want to get pulled over. Jimmy should know better than to talk business with me when I'm driving.

"Look, I tried. He had his little girl with him. She's only five. What was I gonna do? I had to let them go!

It's not her fault! What kind of an asshole would make a little kid pay for what her father did?"

As soon as the words are out of my mouth, I regret saying them. This driving shit is taking way too much of my concentration; I can't think clearly anymore. Jimmy's face darkens, and he scowls at the road, his expression so violent I wonder if he's not going to jump me, no matter what he feels about me. His dad sold him to a brothel to settle a gambling debt when he was seven years old, but that never stopped him from idolizing the man. I don't get it, but Jimmy's real sensitive about it, and he's already made it clear that he resents any implication to the fact that his old man was anything less than perfect.

"I'm sorry, man. I didn't mean anything by it."

"Just drive."

I keep driving for a couple more blocks, but the tense silence and the stupid standard transmission are getting to me, and by the time I'm halfway to my house, I'm really, really pissed off, and gritting my teeth so hard I'm probably grinding off all the enamel. Jimmy sighs, and rolls down his window.

"Just calm the fuck down, already, Alex. It's getting way too hot in here."

I take a deep breath, and try to clear my thoughts. I don't know if it's because I use it all the time, but I've gotten pretty strong lately with this heat thing. I have to be careful when I get pissed off 'cause I make the air around me real hot and, since I don't feel temperature change, I don't notice. It must get cooler, though, 'cause Jimmy doesn't comment again, and he probably thinks it's funny, like he usually does; he doesn't look so pissed off anymore. He grabs my smokes from the inside of my jacket, while I have my hands on the wheel and can't do a thing to stop him, and lights another one. He does it to annoy me; he knows I'm not good enough to do anything else than drive, at the moment, and he usually doesn't smoke in front of me when I can't. He takes a couple of drags, and then clears his throat, picking up the subject like we were never interrupted.

"Anyway, the point is, you're way too soft. I know you don't like it, but everything has its limits, and you can't just keep protecting the hookers and letting guys who owe you money get off easy anymore. The guys are starting to talk, and I'm having trouble keeping a lid on it."

I frown, and nearly miss the stop sign. After starting the engine again, I glance at Jimmy. He's not looking at me, so I go back to watching the road.

"What do you mean?"

"Come on, man. This is costing money. You can't do what we do and be nice to everyone."

"Lupino's nice."

"To you, sure. He likes you. And I'll admit, he's old school, from when mafia meant something more than drugs and hookers. But he didn't make all that money and rise to where he is by bending over for everyone."

I take time to consider it. I don't like to think about it, but I know what he means. I guess by the time I met him he was well established, and everyone doing the dirty jobs was way below him in the ranks.

"What do you want me to do?"

"I told you. Be firm. Don't let things slide. No matter what. If you keep up what you're doing right now, none of the guys will take you seriously anymore, superpower or not. A lot of them are already disrespecting you, calling you soft, some even to my face, and I can't keep covering for you anymore."

I sigh. When I took over from the Borodinski group, it was to protect the kids that had inadvertently fallen under my wing. At first, that's all there was to it, protecting them. Then, I needed to make money, and to defend my territory against groups that would have taken it over for their own. Now that I'm part of Lupino's group, and things have been running smooth for a couple years, I can't pretend I'm just surviving anymore. This is what I do. I have to do it right, or I'm not going to be able to hold it together.

"Fine. Don't worry. I got it."

He nods. He knows I take this seriously, or he wouldn't still be working for me. We don't say anything more until we reach my place.

OCTOBER 5ᵀᴴ, 7:22 PM

The smell of something cooking hits me when I walk into the condo. I get to the kitchen, see there's a frozen lasagna in the oven, but Lori's not there, so I call out.

"I'm home!"

"In here!"

I follow the sound of her voice to Nicolas's room, at the other end of the condo. I stop in the hall and just look at her. She's in her nightshirt. It's too large for her, and it drops all the way to her knees. Her legs and feet are bare under it. She has Nicolas in her arms, and he's pulling on one of the sleeves, yanking it on one side and revealing her smooth collarbone. Her bleached blonde hair is messy, she looks a bit tired, and she's the most beautiful thing I've ever seen, right now, just like that. She notices me, looks up and smiles.

"Hey. Dinner's almost ready."

I walk into the room and kiss the side of her head. She smells like sleep, and I find myself wanting to curl up with her and the baby and just close my eyes. Nicolas is blinking at me. He looks sleepy, too, and I'm about to propose that we all go lie down, but she puts him down in his crib instead. He has a few jerky motions, swinging his fists and his feet in the air, and he concentrates on his mobile. She gestures for me to be quiet, gently takes my upper arm, and leads me out of the room, closing the door behind us. She hugs and kisses me, pushing me against the door, and any thoughts I had of dinner or sleep completely leave my mind. My hands go up to pull her closer, but she breaks our contact, walking away, smiling coyly and running her fingers through her hair.

"I didn't expect you for another half hour. I would have showered."

I take her hand, pulling it away from her hair, and her closer to me. I love it when she has good days. They don't happen very often, they never did, but it reminds me of why I chose to be with her in the first place.

"I don't care. You look wonderful."

She laughs, softly, so she doesn't disturb Nicolas, and gives my hand a tug, resisting my embrace. She lets me go and turns around, heading for the kitchen. I follow her, leaning on the doorframe as she bends to inspect the lasagna through the oven door. Her nightshirt hikes up with the motion, and I can see the back of her thighs. I almost reach out my hand to touch her, but I stop myself at the last second. We both have our issues with being touched, especially her, since she had the baby, and besides, she's opening the oven to pull out the lasagna, and I wouldn't want her to burn herself because of the surprise. She puts it down on the top of the stove, takes off her mitts and turns off the heat. She waves a hand above it, as if to cool it.

"We should wait a couple minutes before eating it, it's still too hot."

I say nothing, just watch her as she pulls a stray strand of her hair behind her ear, before turning to me and giving me a smile that's half-way between embarrassed and confused.

"What?"

I shrug one shoulder, still leaning on the doorframe.

"Just looking at you."

She rolls her eyes, but she's still smiling, and I can see she's not really annoyed at all.

"Oh, come on. I'm not even wearing any make-up, and I'm not dressed."

She doesn't understand, and I don't blame her. She's always needed to look perfect, with sexy, revealing clothes, and she has seduced more men with that look than I care to count. But looking at her like this, I can see the girl I love, the mother of my child, who she truly is under all that fake stuff. It's like a secret treasure, something that no one else can see, or have. I slip a finger in the collar of her nightshirt, and pull her toward me, slowly, to give her a chance to pull away if she wants to. She doesn't, though, and I can see the smile growing slightly on her face as she comes closer. That, more than anything else, hits me in the guts and I want her so bad right now that it feels like my balls are gonna burst.

I grab her upper arms and press her against me, kissing her. Her lips part, and move against mine, and I don't even notice that my hands are moving until I feel the warmth of her thighs in my palms. She presses herself tighter against me, her arms wrapping themselves around my neck. My hands go further up, hiking up her nightshirt, and I've made it all the way to her waist by the time I realize she's not wearing any underwear. I get so hard it feels like my dick is going to rip a hole through the front of my pants. I grab her thighs, and she wraps her legs around me as I lift her up off the ground and bring her to the kitchen table, sitting her on it. She grins at me, her cheeks rosy and her eyes sparkling, her hands moving to unfasten the buttons of my waistcoat. As mine move to the fly of my pants, my phone rings, and I freeze. It's my burner phone, the one I use for work, and I always answer it. It's just never interrupted... a moment like this before. She notices, and has an annoyed sigh.

"You're not going to get that, are you?"

My mouth opens to answer, but no sound comes out, 'cause I have no idea what I want to say. My body wants her so bad, but my stupid brain is making my hand go to my pocket. I manage to stop it from pulling out the phone, though it's really hard. I recognize the ringtone. It's Lupino. The second during which I hesitate is too long, though. Lori snorts and pushes me away, and the moment is gone, as if it never existed.

"Fine. Get your stupid phone. See if I care."

She gets up off the table, walking toward the lasagna. It was only a second. I wasn't going to take that call. Well. Probably not.

"Lori! I..."

"Don't give me that 'it's work' crap again."

"I wasn't..."

"Oh, shut up. Anyway, it's fine. The lasagna's cooled off now. We can eat."

I sigh and say nothing, because I can tell by the way she's banging the cupboards shut that it's not all right at all, but I don't know what she wants me to say, and I know my best bet is just to say nothing. So I sit down at the table and wait for her to drop a plate of lasagna down in front of me. The stupidest thing is, I missed the call anyway, and all this is for nothing.

OCTOBER 6ᵀᴴ, 7:46 PM

Lori hasn't said two words for the entire cab ride. She's not even looking at me. I wonder if she's still mad about yesterday, but I'm afraid to bring it up, because it's one of those things that could make her blow up in my face, and I don't wanna fight with her before we get to mister Lupino's house. Nicolas is asleep in his car seat between us. I reach out and touch his cheek. He fusses and stirs a little, but stays asleep. I look up at Lori to share the moment, but she's ignoring me. I guess she's really pissed off; not talking about it was probably the right call to make. I wish I knew if this was about last night or something else I haven't figured out I did wrong yet.

The cab pulls into the driveway, and she steps out of it to have a cigarette, slamming the door, while I lean forward to pay the driver. I get out of the car with Nicolas in his car seat, and I wait while she finishes her cigarette, staying away from the second-hand smoke. I'm dying to light one up myself, but I swore I wouldn't do it around Nicolas. I never would in front of Lupino's house, either. There's a car that drives by real slow, a black SUV. It attracts my attention because it almost stops in front of the driveway, but then it drives away. Just looking for an address, I guess. I look back at Lori. She's done with her smoke, but she lights another, and I look at the house. It doesn't seem like anyone's noticed us yet, but it's only a matter of time. Besides, I guess I have to talk to her sometime, or dinner will be really, really awkward.

"What are you doing, Lori?"

She rolls her eyes at me. "Playing tennis. What's it look like I'm doing?"

Great. Looks like I was right; she's pissed, not just moody.

"I just mean..." I try to think of the right words, but I don't really know what I mean. I sigh and look towards the house again. "He's waiting for us."

She sighs so loud it's almost like she's shouting, and shakes her head.

"Why did you have to bring me? You know he hates me."

"He does not hate you."

She snorts and raises her eyebrows.

"Well, he thinks I'm not good enough for you."

I open my mouth, and close it. It's true that Lupino has made a couple of subtle comments, but he's never been open about it. He never would. He's too proper. She sees me hesitate, and snorts again.

"Right. Whatever. Call the cab back. I'm leaving."

"Look, Lori, he doesn't know you that well. This is the whole point, he wants to get to know you, see who you are."

"Why does he care, anyway? I mean, does he have to approve of the girlfriend of all the guys who work for him?"

I sigh, and Nicolas starts to wake up, so I bounce his seat a bit.

"No. I guess he doesn't. Just... he and I are close. You know that."

She sighs and shakes her head, throwing the butt of her cigarette in the driveway.

"Give it a rest. He's not your fucking dad!"

My hand suddenly hurts, and there's a smell of burnt plastic. I realize I'm squeezing the handle of Nicolas' car seat so hard my knuckles are white. Who the hell is she to tell me what to do, to pass judgment on my relationship to a man that has made my life so much better? I take a deep breath to calm down, 'cause I don't want to get into a shouting match with my girlfriend where mister Lupino can hear me, and I don't want to accidentally burn anyone, either, especially not my baby boy.

"Ok. That's it. You are going to shut up, get in there, and act like a civilized person through dinner, is that clear?"

She lowers her face so she can glare at me from under her eyebrows, and I can't blame her. I hate the way I sounded just now. But I don't know what to say anymore, and I've seen a curtain move, so someone inside's noticed us. I wanted her along because I thought if Lupino got to know her better, he'd appreciate her a bit. Maybe see a little of what I see in her. But I can see with the mood she's in now, the opposite's probably gonna happen. Since anything else out of my mouth is just going to make things worse, I just turn around and head for the front door, hoping she's going to follow me, counting on her desire to look good, and her insane ability to pretend like nothing is wrong. As I ring the doorbell, I can see her coming up behind me on the porch, and I resist the temptation to cross my fingers. Rosanna answers the door, big smile on her face. I'm sure she's the one who was looking outside, and she knows that we were arguing, but she's pretending that she's not noticed. I wonder if it's something that all women do, or just the ones I know. She embraces me in her arms, kissing both my cheeks, and the smell of bay leaves and the sound of her sweet Italian accent wash off what remains of my anger.

"Alex! It is good to see you. And here is your pretty bambino!"

She leans down towards Nicolas, and coos at him in Italian, unbuckling him from his seat and picking him up. He protests a bit, because he was sleeping, but then he settles down and gurgles happily at her. I don't know if he understands what she says or not, but he's sure been around here often enough that she must be a familiar sight.

"Hi, Rosanna. How is everything?"

"Good! Come in, come in. He is waiting for you."

She shows me inside, ignoring Lori. I look over my shoulder nervously, but Lori has too much pride to let what she's feeling show. Lori and Rosanna have been waging this sort of quiet war between them since they met, for some reason. At least, mister Lupino's more discreet with the way he feels about her, so things could still go smoothly for the rest of the evening. She leads us into the small living room where Lupino keeps all his books and fancy stuff. The picture of his family is still hanging above the fireplace, though now there's the picture of Lori, Nicolas and me that we took at the hospital in a frame on the mantelpiece. He's sitting in one of his comfy chairs, and I can see he's dozed off. I'm about to walk away so I don't disturb him, but Rosanna nudges me forward, nodding, so I go crouch next to him and give his shoulder a gentle shake. He blinks his eyes open, and stares at me in confusion for a few seconds before he rubs his eyes and straightens himself up, smiling at me.

"Alex! I have been expecting you. What time is it?"

I go sit on the other leather chair, across the little coffee table from him. Lori comes in, but only a couple steps, not all the way, like she wants to give us our privacy. More likely, she's pointing out how left out she feels when we come here.

"It's almost eight. I'm sorry, mister Lupino. I'm a little late."

He smiles indulgently, and nods. I hope he's just tired, because his eyes are a little blood-shot, and his face is gaunt. He's not been feeling well for a couple months, now. I hope it's nothing too serious. He turned seventy-five a few months ago. The other capos have started to talk about replacing him, though it's all been hush-hush. They know I'm

Lupino's favorite to take over, we don't really have an official underboss since Jack died, and they all hate me. I know I should do something to sort things out, but I can't bring myself to think about it. I don't know what my life would be like without him.

"Do not worry about the time. At my age, time passes very fast."

I nod, and I take the envelope with my payment out of my pocket, putting it down next to him. He has one small nod to acknowledge it, then looks past me to smile at Lori. I see it, but I hope she doesn't. It's mostly in his eyes, his dislike of her. The way he narrows them, and how his smile doesn't touch them.

"Hello, Lori. How are you doing?"

She smirks, and puts a hand on her hip, leaning on one leg, in that pose she has when she wants to be sexy. He's motioning to another comfy chair, but she doesn't sit down.

"I'm keeping out of trouble, if that's what you mean."

I refrain from sighing. So she's decided to be confrontational. Won't tonight be fun.

"I meant nothing, of course. I just wanted to make sure you are well. Motherhood is challenging, as I recall. Of course, it was a very long time ago."

She opens her mouth to answer, but he just goes on, too quick for her.

"I hope you have brought your son?"

He's looking around. He was really touched that I named my son after his, but he still has a hard time bringing himself to call him by his name. I guess the hurt from losing his family, which was all brought back last year is still too fresh for him. I understand. I don't know what I'd do if something happened to Nicolas, and he's just a baby, not a full grown person with opinions and conversation skills like Lupino's son was.

"He's here. Rosanna's just kidnapped him, is all. I didn't really see where she went."

He smiles.

"She does love him very much. I hope she does not disappear with him all night, like last time. I wish to spend some time with him. How is he?"

"He's great. The doctor said it was almost time for him to start eating real food."

That seems to make him happy.

"Good! Good. I am glad to hear it."

Lori rolls her eyes and sighs, to show how bored she is. Mister Lupino would never show it, but I can see he's annoyed at how impolite she is right now. I wonder why she doesn't even try a little bit. Doesn't she care what people think of her? Especially people that are so important to me?

"I can see your wife is tired. Perhaps we should move to the kitchen."

Lori doesn't comment, and I try to make my face stay neutral. He knows Lori and I aren't married, but he's old-fashioned and Christian, and I think it just makes him feel better to think of her that way, seeing as to how I not only sin with her, but he also really disapproves of her. I'm not sure if it's the fact that she used to be a prostitute, though that's all over. It could be that she was a junkie, but she's been clean for months. She only had the one relapse, after the baby was born, since I got her into rehab when she got pregnant. Then again, it could just be her personality. I have managed to never bring it up so far, and I intend to keep it that way. I hate having confrontations with him.

"Sure. I'm real hungry, anyway."

OCTOBER 6TH, 9:22 PM

Having a baby can be real hard, but at times like these, it can also be a lifesaver. Lori's sour mood almost went unnoticed, seeing as mister Lupino spent most of the meal playing with Nicolas. He didn't eat much. I hope it's only because of the distraction. And after dinner, since Nicolas was getting cranky, it was the perfect excuse for Lori to go home early to put him to sleep, and I got to stay here and have a talk with mister Lupino. He only likes to talk business when it's nice and private, and not even inside the house, so I can tell that's what he's got on his mind when we retire to the garden to have our coffee. Well, I have coffee. He has port wine. He knows I don't drink, and he's stopped offering. When we sit at the small glass table on the stone terrace, though, I can see he's put out the marble chess set he owns, so he expects us to play. I sip my coffee in silence, not looking at him, letting him decide when to start this conversation. I don't really know what he wants to talk about. There could be many subjects, not all of which are comfortable for me, so I've fallen into the habit of letting him lead the conversation. We say nothing for a couple of minutes, and then he turns to look at me.

"How are you enjoying fatherhood?"

I shrug.

"It's all right, I guess. I don't have the difficult part, really. I guess Lori does all the hard work."

He nods, and we stay quiet for a bit longer. That was a pretty obvious attempt to make Lori look good, and he's noticed for sure, but I don't care.

"It was a very honorable thing you did."

I take a moment to think about it, but I'm not sure what he means, though I am sure I don't wanna get into it, so I just nod like I understand. He takes a sip of his port and puts the glass down on the table, next to the chess set.

"And how do you feel about the business, now that you have a family of your own?"

I start frowning at him, but then concentrate on keeping my face blank so he doesn't know how confused I am. What is that supposed to mean? Is he worried I'm gonna bail? Or that I'm not taking things seriously? What am I supposed to say? I try for something neutral.

"Uh... Fine, I guess."

Why do I never realize how stupid some of the things I say are until they're out of my mouth? I clear my throat to give myself a little time to think, and before I realize I'm doing it, I fidget in my seat.

"The, ah, money is sure handy."

The money? Maybe I better shut up. He chuckles, shaking his head.

"Alex, you and I have been through too much together for you to be this uncomfortable with me. Tell me what is really on your mind."

I take a sip of my coffee to think about it. Even if I wanted to say what I really think, I don't know what I think about the business. What does he mean, anyway?

"I'm... not sure what you mean, exactly."

"What I mean is, unlike almost everyone in this line of work, I understand that you have been driven by necessity, not ambition. As I understand it, that necessity is starting to wane."

I nod. I guess he must have heard about Luke registering the house as an official charity. They get a lot more money that way, and access to better care and education than I was able to give them. Still, I don't see what this has to do with anything.

"Sort of... I mean, sure, the kids are taken care of financially, but I still have to make sure they're left alone."

"Oh? Has anyone been after them in the past two years? I was not aware of that."

I do that stupid fish face thing where I open my mouth and close it again. He's right, of course. In the year after I took over the Borodinski group, a lot of people were after them, and what used to be the brothel, but not so much anymore. At first it was because of me and what I could do, and after that, my status and reputation really helped. Now, though... the place is pretty much... off the radar. I'd been so busy with everything I didn't even really think about it.

"...no. I guess not."

He nods once, and smiles at me, looking like he expects me to say something more. I clear my throat again. He's right, but I'm not sure what he wants me to say.

"There's still Lori, and Nicolas. I mean, I have to make money."

"And you cannot do that doing something else?"

I frown, trying not to show how nervous I'm getting. What is he driving at?

"Are you saying you don't want me to work for you anymore?"

He chuckles softly, shaking his head, and reaches over to give me a soft pat on the cheek.

"I enjoy your company more than anyone else's. I think of you as my own son."

He sighs, and takes another sip of his port.

"But I am not sure you have the taste for what needs to be done in this line of work."

I put down my coffee. I feel sick. Is he saying I don't have what it takes? That I'm not good enough? It's true that my numbers aren't as high as when the Russians ran the show. All right, they're nowhere close. I should have listened to Jimmy.

"I'll do better, mister Lupino. I just..."

"You just did what was necessary. And no more."

I open my mouth to speak again, and he raises a hand to stop me, which I guess is a good thing, 'cause I didn't know what to say, and every time I talk without thinking I say something stupid.

"You have a good heart, Alex. You are generous. And kind. You are an honorable man. These are all great, important qualities to have. However, they are not the qualities one needs in the work that we do. One needs to be ruthless. Calculating. Cruel. These things, you are not."

I just stare at him with my mouth open, and I don't even care how I look right now. Is he saying I'm weak? I'm not cut out for this?

"I... I do my best, and I mean... I... I'm young... I can still..."

He smiles, pulling the chess set closer to us.

"I only wish that you take some time to think about it. Your future does not have to be this. And no matter what you choose, you do not have to worry about me. I would not deprive myself of my favorite chess partner."

He takes a white pawn and moves it out on the board, and I put my hand on his to stop him. It's not like the games we play in the park, that are meant to cover up our conversations. Here, we don't let talk disrupt our concentration. So if I want to say what I need, it has to be now.

"Why are you telling me all this, mister Lupino?"

He sighs, but he's smiling, and he lets go of the pawn. He picks up his glass again, and doesn't look at me when he speaks.

"Because I have come to a decision. It probably has not escaped your notice that I am getting old. The... events of last year have left me feeling... tired."

He sips his port, still not looking at me. I know what he means. He hasn't been the same since all that business with his son.

"And so, I have decided that I will be retiring. Not right now, of course. With Jack gone, I need to secure my succession. Which is why I am telling you this now. When I do retire, things will move quickly, and you are not unaware that your position will not be as strong as it is now, while you are still under my wing. You will have to fight to keep it. And I wish to be sure that this is what you really want."

I look down at the chess set. I wish we were playing right now, so I could pretend to concentrate on the game while I try to wrap my head around what's happening. What would I do, if not this? At the same time, do I really want to keep this up if he's not the one I'm working for?

"I... I'll give it some thought, mister Lupino. How long until you... make an announcement?"

He chuckles again. How can he be so relaxed about all this?

"Not for a few months, maybe even a year or two. You have time."

I sigh in relief. A year is a long time. I can come up with some kind of solution by then.

"All right. I think I'm ready to play, now."

OCTOBER 7TH, 12:46 PM

"Come on, little dude, you gotta eat!"

I try giving Nicolas his bottle again, and he opens his mouth to suck on the nipple a couple of times before knocking it away from his face with his hands again. I don't know if he does it on purpose, but one thing's for sure; as soon as it's out of his mouth, he looks at me like it's my fault and starts to cry. I sigh as my phone rings, so I pick it up, welcoming the distraction.

"Hello?"

"Hey boss."

"Jimmy." I sigh with relief. This is probably work, and there's a good chance it's either urgent or important, and that I'll have to go. And leave the baby behind. "Tell me something good."

"I don't really have anything good. I checked into Chris."

"And?"

"And, like I said, it's not good."

"Whatever it is, don't beat around the bush. I got a crying baby here."

I try to balance the phone between my cheek and shoulder to give him his bottle again, but he just keeps turning his head to avoid it.

"Yeah, I hear that. Why isn't Lori taking care of him?"

"I dunno. She's been ignoring him all night and all morning."

"What's the point of being with her if she's not gonna take care of the kid?"

I sigh again. I don't think Jimmy's ever been in a single relationship, at least none that I know about, but I don't think that's any excuse. I mean, I had never been with anyone before Lori, and I still knew why people do it, even if I didn't know how hard it would be.

"What about Chris?"

"Right. So, turns out, he hasn't been stealing money from you. Well. Not exactly."

"What does that mean?"

"Means, his guys are pushing heroin."

I finally manage to get the bottle in Nicolas' mouth again, and he starts drinking. I'm so relieved to have Nicolas finally stop crying, that it doesn't register at first. That, and the fact that I don't know that much about drugs.

"Wait. What? Since when are we pushing heroin? I thought that was the Zhengs."

"We aren't. It is the Zhengs."

"That little cocksucker!"

I'm too loud in my reaction, and it startles Nicolas. He spits out the bottle, and starts crying, spraying me with milk. I take a deep breath to stay calm, wiping my face.

"Yeah. So what do you intend to do about it?"

I hear a challenge in Jimmy's voice, and I know I can't let this slide. I had enough problems with guys betraying me for other groups in the beginning. If it's happening again, then Jimmy's right, and I have been too soft. Even mister Lupino must have heard about it. That's what last night's talk was about. I have to do something about this. Make him an example.

"We take care of it. Today."

"Take care, like look at him sternly and tell him not to do it again?"

I sigh, rubbing my nose. Nicolas keeps crying.

"No, take care of it as in, take care of it. Permanently."

"Fine. I'll pick you up in an hour."

"Make it fifteen minutes and I'll buy you a bottle of... whatever it is you drink."

"It'll have to be twenty minutes. I'm in Old Town."

"What? What are you... oh, never mind. Just get here as fast as you can."

I hang up before he can protest, or worse, explain. He's always in Old Town, lately. At Erik's place. It's not like it's any of my business, anyway. I pick up Nicolas, and walk to the master bedroom. Lori is sitting in bed, smoking a cigarette with the window open. I stop myself from shouting at her, which is really, really hard because I'm already so pissed off, and I really want a cigarette, but we agreed not to smoke inside. At least, I thought we did. She puts it out real quick, and sighs at me.

"What?"

"I gotta go."

I want to add that I had him all night, but I can see she's already in a mood, and honestly, so am I, and I don't want to start anything. She rolls her eyes and sighs exaggeratedly, and stands up.

"Fine. Whatever. Just go."

She comes and picks him up, and I know that she's being difficult on purpose because she wants me to justify myself, or apologize, or change my mind and stay, but she should know better. Besides, it's not like what I'm going out to do is any easier than staying here and watching the kid, and, given the choice, I'd much rather do the latter. But knowing what I'm about to do, it doesn't feel right to be holding my baby boy with these hands.

OCTOBER 7ᵀᴴ, 1:12 PM

I've smoked three cigarettes by the time Jimmy pulls up in front of my building. He turns off the engine and makes to get out of the car, but I don't give him the time to open his door before I slide in on the passenger's side. I can see he's about to protest, and I get ready to argue how much I don't feel like driving right now, but he takes a look at my face and starts the car again.

"Bad day?"

I shrug, lighting up again. I hand him a smoke before he asks, and exhale through my nostrils.

"One of my guys is double-crossing me, I'm fighting with my girl, and everyone seems to agree that I suck at what I do... I've had better."

"I didn't say you sucked. I said you were too soft. And who's everyone?"

I look at him. He's lighting his cigarette, steering with his knee. How does he do that and drive stick? I can't

43

even manage a simple stop without stalling the damn car. I'm about to snap, but then I remember that this isn't his fault. It's true that I'm too soft. Especially since it's not only coming from Jimmy. Even I see it.

I sigh.

"I had a talk with Lupino last night."

"So?"

He doesn't look at me. He doesn't like Lupino; he never has. He always thought we could do better on our own. But he understands that I had to join up, even if he doesn't get how close I got to the man afterwards. Jimmy doesn't get attached.

"So... he's thinking of retiring."

"About time. He's like a hundred years old."

I glare at him, and I try not to shout. He usually knows better than to push my buttons when I'm in a bad mood. Either he's just trying to rile me up, or he's genuinely pissed at me. Either way, I try to calm down.

"He's seventy-five."

"Close enough. Point is, he's ancient."

"Well, that's not the point."

"What is the point?"

"None of his guys like me. They know I'm his favorite, I'm young, I didn't go through all the proper initiations, and I'm not even Italian."

Jimmy gives me a weird look that's halfway between disbelief and disgust.

"He didn't pick you as his replacement, did he?"

"No. Of course not. It's just... he said that..."

I don't know how to say it. I guess I should have thought about it before, 'cause Jimmy gets impatient.

"What?"

"He said he didn't think I was... right for the job. I mean, this job. He said I should consider... getting out before he retires."

Jimmy frowns. Now that I've said it, I realize I'm terrified of what he's going to say. What if he agrees? What if I was never really good at what I do? He knows better than anyone else, better than Lupino, even, what I'm really worth. He's been my right hand man since the beginning. I notice that I'm holding my breath, and try to let it out and start breathing normally again without him noticing. He doesn't seem to.

"I wouldn't go that far. Sure, you need to toughen up a bit, and make sure you don't let people slide so much, but you've been doing pretty good since you started. And yeah, you might be up against pretty big guns if he retires and there's a fight over succession, but you can handle it. I mean, when we started out, we were just a kid and a crazy guy, and we held off everyone way before we had the Lupino group to back us up. And if we have to go solo again, well, whatever. The Winters group has a pretty nice ring to it, doesn't it?"

"Yeah. I guess."

I don't look at him. I guess, to him, there's no question; he loves doing this. He thinks I'm just questioning my ability, and I am, but more importantly, I'm questioning my willingness to do it. I mean, I'm seventeen, and I feel really old and tired sometimes. I don't think I should feel like that at my age, should I?

We reach the old school where Jimmy told Chris we'd meet him. He figured a building about to be demolished would be ideal to cover the traces of what we're about to do, and since it's somewhere Chris is known to hang out at, he won't be suspicious until it's too late. I spot him in the run-down basketball court next to the school. Jimmy parks far enough away from it that Chris doesn't see us at first. He reaches inside his coat, and pulls out a gun and a silencer. As he assembles it, he watches me. I stare at the gun. Thanks to my power, I've never needed to use one. I even stopped carrying one over a year ago. Once the silencer is on, he hands me the gun. I keep staring at it, feeling sick. I've killed people before, with my power, but it's always been in a situation where my life, or somebody else's, was in danger. Not like this. Never in cold blood. Sure, I've scared people into doing what I want, I've beaten up my share of guys, but I've never executed anyone. Seeing that I'm not picking up the gun, Jimmy purses his lips, and sticks it under his seat, silencer and all.

"Fine. I'll do it. It's good enough that you approve. For now."

I can't bear to look at him. As we get out of the car, I see a black SUV park a block away. There's two guys inside, and the driver seems to be looking at me, but when I notice Chris has seen us and is on his way toward us, I put them out of my mind and concentrate on the business at hand. The guys playing around the one remaining hoop stop when they see us, and I think I recognize some of them as members of Chris' gang. I told him to meet here alone. Does he know something's up? Maybe. Then again, he does hang out here once in a while, so maybe that's all it is. He puts his fingers through the chain link fence, leaning over it to talk to us. His eyes are bloodshot, and he looks over his shoulder. He looks paranoid, and he has every right to be; we're here to kill him, after all. I light a cigarette using my power; it always makes me feel like I have the upper hand, which is something I can't afford to lose right now.

"Hey guys! So, uh, you wanted to see me?"

I look at Jimmy, but he's looking at me. Great. Looks like I'll have to do this from the beginning. I guess I really have been relying on him too much, especially lately. I'm the one that should be doing this.

"Yeah. Let's go somewhere more private. We have to talk."

I motion towards the abandoned building, and he looks towards his guys, nervously.

"I don't know... I'm supposed to be meeting with someone about a deal..."

I glare at him. I'm so pissed off right now, I don't even have to make a conscious effort to look scary.

"Oh, I didn't realize we were interrupting something important. Maybe you want to look at your agenda, schedule me when it's more convenient?"

His eyes widen a bit.

"Uh, no, I didn't mean it like that..."

"Then stop wasting my fucking time and get your ass in there."

I start walking towards the building, not looking back, like I know he's gonna follow me. Jimmy falls in beside me, and I sure hope Chris is following, or else we'll have a real problem. But apparently, he hasn't stooped that far into challenging my authority, because he's right behind us when we get in. They've boarded up the windows and doors, but the board that blocks the side door hasn't been nailed down for a while, it just sits there so the squatters can go in and out. Jimmy checked the place out yesterday, and there shouldn't be anyone else in here, but I head to the back just to make sure. There's lots of empty bottles, a few soiled clothes and even the odd sleeping bag, but no one seems to be here, which should make this considerably easier. As easy as it gets, I suppose.

Jimmy finds an old plastic chair and pulls it for me to sit on. We've known each other way too long to stand on formality, but when we're on official business, he insists on it, so I sit, and he stands slightly behind me. Chris looks around, but there's nothing to sit on, so he fidgets. Good. He's intimidated. I stare at him in silence, letting the tension build. He clears his throat and scratches the back of his neck.

"So, um, what's this all about?"

I stare for a few more seconds, and then look over my shoulder at Jimmy. He reaches in the pocket of his coat, pulls out a baggie and throws it at Chris' feet. Chris bends over to pick it up and frowns at it. I cross my legs, and fold my hands over my knee like I've seen Lupino do when he's doing that terrifying calmly unhappy thing he does. Chris turns the baggie over in his hands, and I think I can see his face go white. His eyes are wide when he looks up at us.

"I didn't realize we had started pushing heroin."

"I can explain..."

"I'm listening."

He didn't expect that. He just looks between me and Jimmy, his mouth working soundlessly, like a fish out of water. He obviously has no explanation.

"It... I thought... I could make us more money."

"By working for the Zhengs?"

"I... I'm not!"

Jimmy reaches in his coat pocket again, and pulls out his cell phone, and starts fiddling with it.

"These new phones are great, don't you think? They all come with them camera things. You can take pictures anytime, anywhere."

He turns the phone over to show it to Chris. I take a look, 'cause he hasn't shown me this before. It's in Chinatown, in front of the Mei Fung, where the Zhengs hang out and play Mah Jong. You can clearly see Chris, looking over his shoulder, pocketing an envelope Tony Huang just gave him. I try to keep a lid on my fury. I shouldn't show that I haven't seen this picture before. From the looks of it, though, Chris is way too terrified to notice anything else.

"It's not what it looks like! I just..."

I stand. There is nothing more to be said here, really. Chris' eyes go wide, and he looks between me and Jimmy. I light a cigarette, deliberately, and blow out the smoke before I speak again.

"I have nothing more to say about this, Chris. But I do believe Jimmy has some... words for you."

Chris licks his lips, his eyes so wide he looks like he's losing his mind.

"Boss! You can't do this!"

I turn my back on him, and leave.

"Please, don't leave me with him! Boss!"

I ignore his pleas as I walk to the back of the building. When I step out, I lean on the wall, sighing, putting the hand that's not holding the cigarette over my eyes. I'm shaking, ever so slightly. It might not be me doing the deed, but I just ordered a guy's death. Am I a hypocrite for walking away? I mean, I know Jimmy loves nothing more than to kill a guy, and with someone like Chris, he actually gets to take his time, the way he likes it, but I keep thinking I should have just shot him.

I take another drag from my cigarette, and see movement from the corner of my eye. I frown, and put my hand above my eyes to shield them from the sun. Two dudes are standing there, one in a suit that makes him look like he's in the FBI, and the other in slacker khakis and a black t-shirt.

"Alex Winters?"

I push myself off the wall, frowning, throwing my cigarette to the side. What the hell is it with people seeking me out in weird places, calling me by my full name, lately?

"The hell do you guys want?"

"You're coming with us."

I raise an eyebrow, trying not to squint against the sun. The khakis guy definitely doesn't look like a cop. And even if one of them was, they'd probably have shown a badge, by now.

"No, I'm not. I don't know who the hell you think you are, but I don't scare."

I think for a moment they must be working for Chris, but it doesn't make sense. Wouldn't they know who I was? Why would they need to check? They look at each other in a way I don't like, and then one of them looks at me with a mean expression that I've probably had myself a couple times before, except, like I just said, I don't scare. I smirk at him. If he wants to play intimidation games, he doesn't know what he's up against. He snorts.

"This is your last chance. You come with us, or we're taking you by force."

"Yeah, I'd like to see you try."

"Don't say we didn't warn you."

He claps his hands together loudly, and starts rubbing them. I raise an eyebrow. What is that, some kind of new intimidation meme? I have no idea. I start concentrating on Chris the asshole, but I suddenly feel bad that Jimmy's probably ripping his throat out right now, and it throws me. In that tiny moment, I'm too late. The weird khaki-wearing guy stops rubbing his hands, and waves them at me like he's tossing water, and all of a sudden, there's a weird arc of light shooting from them. I react just in time to dodge it, and it's a really, really good thing I managed it, because it hits the wall behind me, which literally explodes. I cover my head as bits of brick and concrete fall all over me, and as soon as I think I'm no longer in danger of anything big hitting my head, I stand up. As I do, I swing my arm to help me focus, and a wall of fire appears right where they're standing, making them scramble away and giving me time to get all the way to my feet. Before I can do anything else, though, the guy in the suit raises his hands, and all the debris on the ground raises up in the air and flies right at me, hitting me, ripping my suit and the skin under it. I have to raise my arms to cover my face because I'm afraid he's going to take out my eye, and before I know it, something bright hits me right in the gut, sending me flying backwards and into the damaged brick wall. I feel the jagged edges of bricks in my side, bruising and tearing the skin over my ribs, before I fall to the ground. I hear the debris fall, and the khakis guy talking.

"Did we get him?"

I don't move. If they think I'm down, I'm going to use that to my advantage. As they observe me from afar, I concentrate on everything that pisses me off. How cocky these guys are. How Lori keeps being so hot and cold with me. How my guys are starting to turn on me. By the time they start moving towards me, carefully, to check if I'm really down, I'm ready.

They're three feet away when I strike. I know from the experience I have fighting a bunch of bloodsuckers that if I'm quick and hot enough, I can reduce a body to practically ashes in a matter of seconds. I go for half that heat. I don't think they're trying to kill me, and I don't really want to start leaving a bunch of dead, burned bodies in my wake; not at something that's going to be a potential crime scene, and not when the cops are already trying to find a way to pin three fires on me. Still, the blast I engulf them in is hot enough to make them scream much higher than any grown man should be able to. I scramble to my feet, and run for the door. Before I duck in, I can see that one of them is on the ground, rolling to put out the fire, and the other one, though he's managed to extinguish it, is hurt badly enough that he's going to need serious and immediate medical attention.

This should give me time to get Jimmy and get the hell out of here.

I run inside, and almost all the way to the room we were sitting in a moment ago. Before I get in, I slow down, to collect myself in case Jimmy isn't done. When I pass the threshold, I'm reminded of the reason people call Jimmy 'Blood Bath'.

There is blood everywhere. It's splattered on the walls, the ceiling, and it's pooled on the floor in three different places. There are bits of bloody flesh lying in them, around Chris' body, and I see that part of his face is mangled beyond recognition, one of his eye sockets is bloody and empty, and his throat is so ripped up I swear one of the bits lying next to him has to be his windpipe. I look away, gagging, and I try to take a deep breath but then the smell hits me, and I lose my lunch right there.

"Ah, don't be a pussy, boss."

I jump, wiping my mouth, and turn. I hadn't seen him at first, and I thought he had left, but Jimmy is slumped into a corner, a hand pressed on his side. I can see that he's covered in blood; face, hair, jacket, t-shirt, and especially his hands, which look sticky all the way up to the elbows. There's something weird about his posture, though. Usually, this kind of carnage is something that makes him hyper, and energized, but now, he simply looks beat, weak, like he doesn't have the strength to stand up. I squint at him, and I realize that there's something wrong with the blood that's covering him. If it's all splatters from Chris, how can there be this much on his t-shirt, which is under his jacket?

"Jimmy? Are you bleeding?"

He raises an eyebrow at me.

"Yeah, I'm bleeding. Fucker stabbed me in the gut. I hate being stabbed. I put out his eye, though. That'll teach him."

I try not to look over at Chris, because being sick in front of Jimmy once was enough. He sighs, looking down at his gut. Why is he so calm? I go over to him, quickly, but with no rush, so he can't tell I'm worried out of my mind. Is he dying?

"Are you ok?"

He rolls his eyes.

"No, I'm not ok, dumbass, he stabbed me. Aren't you listening? Sheesh. Your old lady's got something when she complains about how you don't listen, you know."

I kneel down, and start to lift his jacket to take a look at the wound, but he bats my hands away.

"Ah, don't touch me. I don't want no one mothering me. I'm gonna be fine."

I frown.

"You sure?"

"Yeah, I'm not coughing blood, so he didn't touch my lung, and it's too high to be one of those fatal gut wounds, so I just gotta wait it out."

"I'm taking you to a hospital."

"No, you're not. You're going to help me stand and you're gonna take me to Erik."

I blink at him.

"What?"

He sighs audibly, rolling his eyes again.

"Fucking hell, boss, you gonna make me repeat everything? I'm not that high on energy, here. You're taking me to Erik's place. He knows a guy."

"And you know that how?"

"Ugh. Look, I've been stabbed often enough to know I haven't been hit anywhere vital, but that don't mean I got all the time in the world to just sit here and chat. Are you gonna take me, or should I break out the whiskey so we can have a chat while I bleed to death?"

I sigh, but grab him by the upper arm and help him stand.

"Fine. But I don't know how advisable it is to show up at a vampire's place all covered in blood."

He limps next to me, and shrugs.

"He's all right. We got a thing. An understanding thing."

"Suit yourself. But if he starts licking you, don't say I didn't warn you."

OCTOBER 7ᵀᴴ, 1:49 PM

The house looks as shabby as I remember it. I know the guy can't come out in the daytime to fix it up, but shit, I should really tell him it's an eyesore. I have to practically carry Jimmy inside. He's losing a lot of blood, but he's still conscious, and I know he'll argue about me taking him to a hospital if he's not passed out. I bang on the door.

"Erik! Open up! Erik!"

There's no answer, so I just try the door. It's not locked, so I walk inside, half dragging Jimmy. His head is rolling on his shoulders, so I check his face, but his eyes are still fluttering, so I yell.

"Erik! Get your ass down here!"

"What?"

He appears at the top of the stairs, wearing happy-face boxers and a Big Bird t-shirt. I look at him for a second, and then walk to the living room to drop Jimmy off on a couch. Jimmy moans a bit, and then tries to sit up. I kneel next to the couch.

"Don't move, man."

He bats my hands away, sitting up anyway.

"Don't touch me. I told you I was fine. Leave me alone, and gimme a cigarette."

The hand he holds out is smeared in blood, and a little gore, and I frown, thinking his wound must be worse than I thought, but then I remember Chris and feel sick again. I take out my cigarette case and hand him a smoke as Erik, not any more dressed than he was a moment ago, comes in, scratching his ass and yawning.

"What the hell are you... oh."

He blinks at Jimmy, and then yawns again.

"I thought I smelled lunch. What happened?"

Jimmy mumbles while fumbling with his Zippo to light himself up.

"Shut up, cocksucker. Call your guy, will ya?"

Erik shrugs, and reaches for the small paper phone book next to his rotary-dial phone. Seeing that Jimmy's hands are too slick with gore to get the mechanism on his lighter working, I hold out my hand and make some fire.

"Here you go. Are you sure you're gonna be ok?"

He takes the time to light his cigarette before answering me.

"Sure. Go to the kitchen, there's some towels under the sink. Bring me a couple, and a beer from the fridge."

I raise an eyebrow, because I'd really like to know how the hell he knows all that about Erik's kitchen, but it's really not the time, and I think that deep down I really don't wanna know, so I just get up and go get him what he needs. When I come back, Erik is hanging up the phone, and looking at Jimmy.

"He's on his way. He'll be here in a few minutes. Think you're gonna make it?"

Jimmy shrugs.

"Hell, if I don't, I've had a good run, right?"

Erik shakes his head, leaning back down on his couch.

"Well, at least if you croak I'll have something to snack on."

I sit next to Jimmy, though I'm careful not to get any blood on me, and I'm about to press the towels into his wound, but he just grabs them and does it himself, grinning at Erik, barely acknowledging me.

"Not if I bleed to death. What'll you do, lick it off the floor?"

Erik frowns, thinking about it.

"Didn't think about that. Maybe I can cancel my guy and just finish you off now."

They look at each other and just chuckle. I shake my head. I really don't get them, but I guess they get each other. I look at Jimmy. He's still losing blood, and I can't resist the urge to turn to Erik.

"Your guy, he's a doctor?"

Erick shrugs.

"Sorta. He'll help."

I turn towards Jimmy, who rolls his eyes at me.

"Stop fussing, man, you're like ten times worse than Luke. Go get yourself a beer, or something, just chill out."

I snort, and stand up. I don't want a beer, but I'm already standing, so I have to do something. Besides, it is stressing me out, and I know that I shouldn't stress Jimmy cause it'll make his heart pump faster and he'll just bleed out quicker. I go to the kitchen, but I don't even open the fridge. I just stand there, leaning against the counter, listening to them joke around. I can't hear what they say, but they seem to think it's all pretty funny.

Lupino's right. I'm not cut out for this life.

There's a knock on the front door, and I practically run to the door. Eric beats me to it, though, and he has to step aside to keep out of the light when he lets in an old guy with a scraggly beard and a plaid flannel shirt carrying what looks like a toolbox. Neither of them says anything, and I follow them to the living room.

Jimmy looks passed out, his head leaning back on the couch, his mouth hanging open. Erik is leading in a guy with a big plastic case.

"He's here. Can you help him?"

The guy frowns, looking worried, and looks down at Jimmy.

"How long has he been unconscious?"

Jimmy's head moves slightly, and he coughs.

"...m'not unconscious."

"That's good. Is all that blood yours, son?"

Jimmy moves his leg weakly, as if to kick the guy, and then just sighs.

"...m'not your son."

I roll my eyes.

"No. A lot of it is someone else's. Is he going to be ok?"

The guy shrugs, getting to work cleaning the wound.

"It looks like. Just get some iron and fluids into him. He should really be in the hospital, though. I have no way to tell if he needs a transfusion."

"Fine. We'll think about it next time. For now, though, just make sure he's all right."

I sit down on the opposite couch, and watch the guy work on my best friend.

OCTOBER 7ᵀᴴ, 6:57 PM

The taxi drops me off in front of my building, and I climb up the steps slowly. In front of the door, I stop, take out a cigarette, and light it. My phone beeps again, and I don't even have to check it to know it's a text message from Lori. She's the only one that texts me, and she's been wanting me to come home for two hours now. I sit down on the steps as I smoke. This has been a long, long day, and I need to wind down before I come in and face whatever mood Lori's going to be in. It was bad enough that I needed to see and hear the guy sew up Jimmy's gut without anesthesia, but when he was gone, all Jimmy wanted from me was my smokes and for me to go away. Then I had to wait for the cab outside, not even sure if he was going to live through the night or not. Someone walks in front of the stairs, and I jump up to get ready to fight, but it's just my neighbor, carrying a bunch of shopping bags. He starts, and blinks at me as I sit back down, sighing and lighting another cigarette. I try to ignore him, but he raises an eyebrow, looking me up and down so obviously it's almost loud.

"Rough day?"

I glare at him, because I want to tell him off and I don't really know how to put it. I suppose he does have every right to stare. My suit is all torn up and stained with blood. He looks like he's about to say something more for a minute, and then shakes his head and walks inside. I sigh, throw the butt of my cigarette away, and get up to walk in after him. I let him ride the elevator up to our floor and take the stairs just so I can be alone. I'm wheezing by the time I'm on the fourth floor; guess maybe I should cut back a bit more.

I walk in, and before I've taken two steps in, the bathroom door opens and Lori steps out. Her hair is all mussed up, and she's wearing make-up and a red nightie that reminds me of the day I met her. She walks toward me, swinging her hips. Seems she's been expecting me, even though I haven't answered any of her texts. Maybe I should have. I'm a little relieved, cause she seems to be in a good mood, but I'm cautious. She hasn't put on makeup in a long time, and there's something off. I close the door behind me, and by the time it's locked, she's reached me, and is staring at me.

"Ew. What happened to you?"

I sigh, removing my jacket.

"Job. Got complicated."

I don't want to scare her with the superpowered guys, so I don't say anything about that. She knows enough about what I do to assume I got in a fight, and I'm sure that's good enough for both of us. She puts her arms around my neck.

"Aw... Sounds like you had a rough day. I can make it better."

I smile. She really is in a good mood, it seems, and she doesn't look high. I lean down to kiss her, and the smell hits me like a wall. Looks like today's been a bad day for her, too. I pull back and push her away before I realize what I'm doing.

"You reek! Have you been drinking?"

She pulls back and sighs, throwing her hands up in the air.

"You are such a killjoy! You want to take away everything that makes me happy? What's wrong with a little wine, huh? It's not like I got high or anything! Why can't you just be happy and leave me alone?"

I don't mean to, but I check her arms for track marks. She notices me, of course, and she clicks her tongue.

"So what, now I'm a liar? Well here, check it out!"

She shows me the folds of her arms, and I feel ashamed when I see that, of course, they're clean. I look down and step toward her, ready to apologize. I guess it's true that I shouldn't mind her drinking a little, even if on her breath, it smells like a whole lot. I just wish she didn't do any of those things. I think about what to say to make it right, and put my hand on her cheek. She seems to ease up, ready to forgive.

"Lori, I..."

Then I hear Nicolas cry, and it's coming from the living room. It shouldn't be coming from over there. I step away from her again, and I don't even care about her exaggerated sigh anymore. I almost fly to the living room, and when I see him, my heart jumps, and I flip. He's crying, and kicking his legs slightly. In fact, it's good I came in now; he's partially off the couch, head hanging over the edge. She's just left him there, with nothing to prevent him from falling. I pick up my baby boy, and he settles down almost instantly, glad for the attention.

"Shh, Nicky boy, daddy's got you."

His little hand reaches behind my head and finds my ponytail, pulling. He loves to pull my hair. I let him, turning to face Lori as she comes in behind me. I think she can see the fury in my eyes, 'cause there's a little shame in her annoyance.

"What?"

"What? What? Are you serious? You don't leave a five month old baby alone on the couch! What were you thinking? He almost fell! He would have fallen on his head, too, he could have died!"

She shrugs.

"He's fine! It's no big deal; I do it all the time. I just went to the bathroom."

"This is why you can't drink!! You're in charge! I have tons of things I have to do, I can't be around here all the time, and you're responsible for him! Don't you understand?"

She shakes her head and walks to the kitchen. Nicolas has started crying again. He hates it when we fight, and it seems to happen more and more lately. I make a shushing sound in his ear; that always seems to soothe him, and it's no different today. I hear the sound of the fridge door opening, and a glass bottle being retrieved. I don't want to hear it, so I retreat to the baby's room. I put him down in his crib, and turn on the little mobile. He fusses a bit, but he hears the music, he calms down, and his eyes blink open to follow the brightly colored fish going in a circle above his head. He reaches a hand up to bat at them. It's something he's been doing for months, now, but I'm not bored of it yet, so I watch him go at it for a few minutes, though of course, the fish are too far and he can't reach them. He makes a few little frustrated sounds, but as always, he just tries harder. I lean down to pat his head. I'm still awkward with him. I've never been good with physical affection, and I sure don't know how good parents are supposed to be, but I want it to be different with him. I hear something crash in the hall, and I sigh, walking away from my son. At least, for all I'm not sure about, I'm nearly an expert at how parents aren't supposed to be.

I walk out of the room before she makes it there, and I close the door behind me. She has a bottle of white wine in her hand and an angry look on her face. This smells like another fight, and I try to dodge it and her to head toward the bedroom. She tails me all the way there, and I try not to say anything that will spark it. I'm so tired of fighting with her; and here I actually thought this was going to be a good evening. She sits on the bed and drinks while I take off my jacket and waistcoat and give them a sorry look before tossing them in the trash. Another expensive suit ruined. Maybe I should start buying cheap. I've had to buy a lot since my house burned down last year. At more than a thousand bucks a suit, it shows, even when you make the kind of money I do. I also have to throw out my tie, pants, and shirt. The only thing that didn't get damaged beyond repair is my belt, so I hang that on the back of the chair. I start to look at her, and I'm almost relieved to see that her eyes are glazing over with the haze of alcohol. I hate dealing with anyone when they're drunk, but I'm not sure if I'd rather have her pissed off.

"What the hell happened to you, anyway?"

I sigh. I didn't really want to trouble her with it, but I'm really glad for the distraction, and with how drunk she is, it's a good bet that she won't take it seriously enough to worry, anyway.

"Got into a fight with a couple guys."

"Looks serious."

"Well... it was more weird than anything else. They could... do things."

"Things?"

"The kind of things I can do."

She snorts in laughter.

"Really? So what, are they some kind of superheroes? Does that make you a supervillain?"

I try to smile. Seems like she's getting back into a good mood. Maybe I can escape the inevitable fight after all. I pull on a t-shirt, and when I turn back to her, she's drinking from the bottle. It's almost empty; she must be pretty far gone. I try to push my rage down, breathing in through my nose. I keep telling myself that this is better than fighting. Isn't it? She stands up, and walks over to me as I'm looking for some sweatpants through the mess of unfolded clean clothes that are just thrown over my drawer, blocking it open. Her hands wrap around my waist and she puts her cheek against my shoulder blade as I stand all the way back up. I've grown in the last year, a lot; she used to be able to lean her chin on my shoulder without standing on tiptoes. Now, she's a lot shorter than I am. I wonder if I'm done growing yet; I know she is, and has been for a few years, but then again, she's a few years older than I am.

I feel her lips on my skin, and I try to get in the mood. This is a lot better than fighting, anyway. Even if she is drunk. I have to push down my anger too, but it's a lot easier with her than with anyone else. Even with the way she treats my son. Our son. He's so small, and helpless, and she's the only one that can take care of him... But I can't think about that. It just makes me angry again. I know; I'll bring him to Luke in the morning. He's good at looking after kids. He's never looked after one this young, or at least I don't think so, but the decision is already making me feel better, and I can let go of my anger at last.

OCTOBER 8ᵀᴴ, 10:39 AM

The taxi pulls into the driveway of the house, and as I pick up the car seat and the heavy, full bag that I have to carry every time I take Nicolas anywhere, I see a couple of faces appear in the window. I spot Kim running back into the house almost immediately, and I hurriedly unstrap Nicolas' car seat.

Before I have the time to get to the house, the door bursts open and Kim runs out, wearing fluffy slippers, pink pajamas and a Disney Princess bathrobe. I barely have time to put down Nicolas' seat before she throws her arms around me, and I pick her up, giving her a twirl. She giggles when I put her back down.

"Alex! You've come to visit!"

I'm about to answer when she notices the seat on the ground, and squeals.

"Oh! You've brought your little baby!! Can I hold him, please?"

73

I smile at her and nod. She reaches down and carefully unclasps the restraints holding him in place. He startles himself awake, and starts to fuss a little, but settles down when she wraps her arms around him. I resist the urge to tell her to be careful. I know she will be, and she's held him lots of time before. Besides, if I can bring myself to trust Lori to be alone with him all day, I can trust Kim to carry him inside the house while I'm supervising her.

Luke meets us at the door and smiles down at Kim as she proudly shows him the baby.

"Look, Luke! He's getting big, isn't he?"

He nods.

"Sure is. What are you feeding this kid, Alex?"

I blink. His face is serious, and it's hard to tell if he's kidding or not. Suddenly, I'm having doubts. Should I be feeding him something special?

"Well. Formula."

He slaps my upper arm.

"Don't be so serious. Come on in, I'll make some coffee. Kim, you be careful with him!"

She frowns at him, looking deeply offended.

"I am!"

"Leave her alone, Luke, she's all right."

She grins at me before heading to the living room, where I can hear the other girls gather around her and start to coo at the baby. I pick up the bag and follow him in. I'm glad he finally redecorated since the fire. It doesn't look like the brothel it used to be anymore, but it does look a little like a community center. What used to be the smaller living room is now full of tables for games, like foosball, air hockey, and ping pong.

Luke leads me in the kitchen, where I sit down at the counter. He's changed everything in here too, so it looks more like a commercial kitchen. I can see he's added a second oven, and two microwaves. With all the kids that live here, I guess it can't be too much. I wouldn't know. I never cook, and neither does Lori.

He pours me a cup of coffee and slides it to me without adding anything in it, before pouring himself a mug, adding milk and sugar so that it's hardly coffee anymore.

"You're not here for a visit, are you."

I start to act offended, then just sigh. Luke doesn't beat around the bush when there's something on his mind, and he always knows what's going on with everyone. Sometimes I wonder if he can read thoughts. I mean it's probably possible, after all I can manipulate fire with my mind, and with what happened yesterday obviously other people can do weird stuff too, but I've never met anyone who could do something like that.

"No. Can you watch him for the day? I got things to do. I'll take him off your hands tonight, I swear."

He shakes his head.

"He can stay here for as long as you want, there's no need to worry. It's you I'm wondering about. What's going on? Did Lori..."

He doesn't finish, but I know what he's asking. After all, Lori did live here with us for years before we bought the condo. I shake my head.

"No, she didn't relapse. She's fine."

"Mmhmm."

He takes a sip of his coffee, watching me over the rim of his glasses. Luke is probably the only person that can make me feel uncomfortable just by looking at me. Well, except for mister Lupino. Even Jimmy doesn't know how to do that, and I know what Jimmy's capable of. Thinking of Jimmy makes my chest feel tight. I hope he's all right. I wouldn't really know what to do without him. I try to get back to the matter at hand.

"I just wanted to give her a break, that's all."

"Right."

He keeps looking at me. Why does he keep looking at me? I don't get why it's so important to him that I talk about my feelings. Are they relevant to his willingness to watch over my kid?

"What?"

"Tell me what's going on, Alex. You know I can help."

I sigh. I hate that he's right, but he is. He can usually help.

"It's nothing. It's just... Lori has a hard time, that's all."

"How much of a hard time?"

I shrug. I don't like talking about it. It makes me feel like a bad father that I'm not taking better care of both her and the baby. I know she has her problems, but she shouldn't feel like that. I should help better.

"You know... she drinks a lot. Sometimes I come home and I don't like where she's put the baby. Or he's howling and she's doing nothing about it. Or you know... stuff."

"It's hard to deal with having a baby. And she's had... circumstances."

I nod. I know she's not all there emotionally. And I know she's had problems. Not just the drugs, but her whole past, which probably includes more than just her time here. She never talks about her parents, or what they were like, but they have to have been as bad as mine for her to end up in a place like Mikov's brothel.

"I know, Luke. I just don't want Nicolas to grow up to be as fucked up as we are."

"He won't, don't worry about it. We're not our parents, and the big difference with you is that you actually care. You can't go wrong when you do that. Besides, give yourself a little time to learn. I know you don't like to be reminded,

77

but you're barely seventeen. You'll get better. You both will. You can't be perfect, and even if you could, it wouldn't be in just a couple of months."

I glare at him. He knows I don't like it when people mention my age; besides, he's not that much older than I am, so he doesn't have to act all superior about it. My phone rings, and I see that it's Jimmy. My heart jumps, and I pick up right away, no matter how rude that is.

"Jimmy?"

His voice sounds slurred, and I find myself actually hoping he's been drinking.

"Hey, boss. How're you?"

"Fine. How are you? Are you ok?"

"Yeah, yeah, I'm gonna be fine. You wanted me to call when I was feeling better, so I'm calling."

"All right. I'm on my way."

"There's no need. I'm really feeling ok."

"Well, I'm coming anyway."

"Fine. Whatever. Give us at least half an hour."

"Uh, no problem."

I try not to think about it as I hang up, and look up at Luke.

"Sorry, Luke. Gotta go. Call me if there's anything."

"Everything ok?"

"Yeah. Jimmy got hurt pretty bad yesterday."

Luke frowns, looking halfway between shocked and confused.

"How bad? I mean, he's been hurt quite a few times in his life, he's always been ok."

I make a face.

"Pretty bad. He's been stabbed."

Luke waves a hand, dismissive.

"He'll be fine. He gets stabbed all the time."

I shake my head. Luke's known Jimmy for a really, really long time, ever since they were both kids, and he seems to think Jimmy's invincible. I have to admit that even I think that Jimmy's invincible.

"I guess. Just... give me a call if there's anything, will you? You have my new number?"

"You didn't change it since last week?"

I change phone numbers pretty often, because I use burner phones. I used to have a phone with a plan, for personal calls, but since I got a home phone, I dropped it.

"No, it should be the same. Anyway, Lori has it, so if you can't reach me, call her. But only if you can't reach me, ok?"

"Sure."

I pretend not to see the smile that says he'll call her anyway, and walk out. I'm tempted to go check on the girls and the baby, but I'm in too much of a hurry. Besides, it's irrational for me to miss Nicolas right away when I leave him somewhere. I mean, he's just a baby. I didn't think I'd be so attached so fast.

I light a cigarette when I walk out, grabbing my cell phone and calling another cab. As I hang up, I notice two guys making their way toward me. I frown at them, watching them come, but they don't seem threatening or official, so I wait and see what they want. I'm cautious, and I prepare to get into a fight, but there's no use starting something before I know what they want. One of them is a short guy with a wool turtleneck and a hat, and the other one is a tall, round dude with a Black Sabbath t-shirt. They could just be walking by, too, though I get the impression they're coming for me. The short guy smiles at me, friendly-like, so I relax a bit. They'd be more business-like if they wanted to pick a fight. He takes a pack of cigarettes from his pocket, getting one out and putting it in his mouth, and gestures at me with his chin.

"Hey, man, got a light?"

I consider it for a while, and then I hold out my finger, flame at the tip of it. If they had any notion of doing me harm, I can at least try to impress them, and make it really clear that it's not a good idea to mess with me. I frown as the

80

guy doesn't even blink, but just reaches to take my wrist and stabilize it so he can lean down to light his cigarette. As he's about to light up, he suddenly looks up at me and smirks. I'm about to ask him what the hell his problem is, but then I feel something being drained from me, and the fire goes out from my finger. I'm so startled, all I can do is stare at my hand stupidly for a few seconds, giving enough time for the big one to raise his hand in a weird hand gesture, like he's casting a spell on me. I'm about to ask him what his problem is, when I feel the air being sucked from my lungs, and I can't speak, I can't even breathe. I turn and start to run away, but I don't manage to get very far because my chest feels like it's imploding, and my vision is getting blurry, and there's darkness at the edge of it. I don't know how far I manage to run, but I know I pass out before I hit the ground.

DATE AND TIME UNKNOWN - DAY 1

It takes me forever to wake up all the way. My whole body feels heavy, I can't see right, and it's a long time before I can sit up. I'm in a small room that looks a bit like a hospital room. It's kind of lifeless, even sterile. The bed is one person sized, with a light green wool blanket and white sheets. The floor, walls and door seem to be made of some kind of weird ceramic, and there's a huge mirror that looks more like a window on the wall, a small metal toilet on another wall, and nothing else. I search my pockets. Whoever they were, they took everything. I don't have my cell phone, my keys, my wallet, or my cigarettes anymore.

I rush to the door, but of course it's locked. I can feel panic rising up in my chest and try to push it down; it's not very conducive to me using my power. It's hard, though; the last time I woke up in a strange, locked room, I was trapped in Mikov's brothel, and things did not go well. Not for a good long while, anyway. I manage to get a hold of myself, and put both my hands on the handle. At least my power's back; I can feel the fire surging from my hands, hammering at the door, and the wall, but the lock still holds. I try it long and hard enough for the room to get so hot that the clothes on

83

my back are starting to singe, even catch fire. Same with the bed. I even start to sweat, which is pretty rare. Yet the door and the walls seem completely unaffected. The panic is back; it's rising high enough to push the anger out of my blood, making my fire go away. In minutes, I'm reduced to screaming and pounding on the door with all my might.

"Let me out! Let me out! You can't do this! Let me out!!"

My screaming is so frantic that I don't hear it for a couple of minutes, but as I get winded and fall to my knees in front of the door, I notice that there is a pounding on the wall to my right, and I can make out a voice.

"Stop it, you idiot!! You're gonna roast me alive!"

I stare at the wall, and notice a small vent at the top of it. With it being hot enough to singe linen in here, it must be unbearable for any normal person on the other side of that vent. But I'm too pissed off to really care, right now.

"Who are you? Where am I?"

"Finally! Can you make it not so hot anymore?"

"Not until I get some answers!"

"Fine! I'm Julie. You're at GenEx. Now can you make the heat go down, please?"

"Can you get me out of here?"

"God, how much of a dumbass are you? If I could get you out of here, I would have gotten myself out of here, and

84

I wouldn't stay here swimming in buckets of my own sweat! Now bring the temperature back to normal!"

I close my eyes to better concentrate. Bringing the temperature down is something I can do, but it's difficult in the best of circumstances, and I'm not exactly at my top mental capacity here. It feels like forever before I can manage it, and being insensitive to temperature change, I have to ask.

"Is it better?"

"It's not great, but it's better."

"I don't suppose you'd know a way to get out of here?"

"What, do I have to repeat myself? I'm a teleporter. Trust me, there is no way out. If they brought you here, it's because they know how to keep you here. End of story."

I sit on the bed and put my head between my hands. I think of Nicolas, at Luke's place. Luke. He'll be expecting me back. What's gonna happen to my kid if I don't get out of here? Would Luke just bring him back to Lori? What's she gonna do if I don't get back to her? Is she gonna be ok with Nicolas on her own? What if she relapses again? What about my work? Will Jimmy be ok? Will he know what to do while I'm gone? And what about Lupino?

"You ok, kid?"

How does she know how old I am? My voice finished shifting years ago!

"I'm not a kid!"

"Well, you don't sound that old. How old are you?"

"It's none of your business!"

"So, you're a kid then. And your power is heat. What's your name?"

"Why do you care?"

"I've had nothing better to do than to just sit here for weeks, now. My guess is, you won't have much better to do for a while, either. Might as well have someone to talk to."

I look at the vent. I hate talking on the phone, and this isn't much better, but whoever she is, I guess she's right. Besides, I could use an ally, or at the very least, some company.

"I'm Alex. So... my power works, obviously. How come yours doesn't?"

"Huh?"

"You said you were a teleporter. Wouldn't you be out of here already?"

"They've got some kind of weird electromagnetic field that disrupts my ability. That's all I know about it. Don't really know how it works, just that it keeps me from teleporting."

"Oh. So..."

I'm cut short by the door to my cell opening, and I jump to my feet. Whoever's coming in, they've got the key, which means their ass is going to be fried in a couple seconds. I see two men walking in, and one of them is the greasy-haired fuck who came to sit at my table at the café the other day. I'm definitely pissed enough to make enough heat to reduce them to ash on the spot, but for some reason, when I summon the fire, it doesn't come. It feels like it's just gone, like it did on the street. What's happening to me? Am I losing my mind, or my power? Right now, I'm not sure which would be worse.

"How nice it is to see you again, mister Winters. I'm sorry the circumstances aren't better ones, but unfortunately you have left us no choice."

The guy with the greasy hair, Finley, I think, gives me his snake's smile, and motions to his companion, a gray-haired skinny guy with dead eyes.

"Alex Winters, meet my colleague, Harvey Edgars. He will be your mentor during your stay at GenEx Facilities. You will find that in his presence, you will not be able to make use of your fire."

The older guy has the affront to nod at me, like he's casually introducing himself.

"What the hell do you want from me?"

The greasy snake shrugs.

"Simply what I said earlier. We hope to find out more about what you can do. And we will teach you how to better use your power."

"What the hell for? I told you I wasn't interested! What the hell do you hope to gain from keeping me here against my will?"

"Well, for starters, we hope to prove to you that there is no need to be so contrary. This cell is meant to prevent you from escaping, that is correct, but once you become cooperative, you will be free to walk about the entire compound, and when you have proven your loyalty to us, you will be free to come and go as you wish."

"You're sick! You can't just treat people that way!"

He has a small smile, and turns his back on me, like I'm no threat at all.

"In time, you..."

He doesn't have time to finish, because I jump right on him, tackling him to the ground and punching his head with all I've got. The other guy is surprised for a second, but by the time he's trying to pull me off, greasy snake is good and stunned, and I can start wailing on Harvey, too. Neither of them seems to have much hand-to-hand experience. They have grossly underestimated me, much to my advantage; just because I don't have my powers doesn't mean I'm helpless. I punch him square on the nose, and before he's recovered his wits, I kick him in the stomach, pushing him away from me. I run toward the door, and straight into a huge guy, hard enough to make me bounce back a couple of steps. He seems completely unfazed, though, and just lifts an eyebrow at me. He's gotta be at least a good head taller than me, and twice my weight, but I've fought full-grown men as a boy, so he doesn't scare me. I punch him across the face hard enough to hurt my fist, and when that leaves him unmoved and unimpressed, I try kicking him in the groin. He just looks down at my foot like it's a funny little thing, then picks me up by the shirt like I'm weightless, and throws me hard across the room. I hit the wall so high I think I bounce of the ceiling before falling to the ground, and my head spins when I try to stand up. Finley the greasy snake is standing back up, Harvey is holding his bleeding nose, and they're both glaring at me like I'm the one who's out of line.

Finley brushes imaginary dirt off his cheap suit, and looks at me with an annoying sneer.

"I certainly hope you've understood the futility of trying anything of the sort again. I do believe we should let you think about what you've done for a little while before we come back for you. That was terribly ill-behaved of you."

He pulls on the lapels of his jacket as if to adjust them, gives his left sleeve one final brush, and turns to walk away, followed by the two other guys. The door closes behind them, leaving me alone with my misery. I hear Julie's voice on the other side, asking me if I'm ok, but I don't feel like answering, and I just curl up on my singed bed. I feel defeated right now. Trapped. It brings back really unpleasant memories; I haven't felt like that since I was fourteen years old. I know I'll get other chances, but I don't want to talk about it with some stranger through an air vent.

DATE AND TIME UNKNOWN - POSSIBLY DAY 2

I barely sleep that night. At least, I think a night went by; it's hard to tell. Almost all the cloth burned off the bed, and I'm mostly lying on metal springs. When I wake up, my head feels like it's three times its normal size, and I groan as I sit up. The lights are still on; I don't know if that means it's still the same day, or if they just don't turn them off.

Julie calls out to me from her cell.

"You finally awake in there?"

"Ugh. Yeah."

"What happened?"

"They were getting cocky with me. I tried to kick their ass."

"Oh. Bet that didn't work, did it?"

"Not so much. Made one of them bleed, though."

"Yeah, they never go in a cell without having Will nearby, at the ready. He's the big dude. He came in, didn't he?"

"If he hadn't, I would be out of here by now."

"Well, kudos for trying, kid."

I sigh. I'm too tired to even try and argue with her about it anymore. Then something hits me.

"You know this place pretty well, don't you?"

"What makes you say that?"

"The big guy… You called him by name. How long have you been here, exactly?"

"Here, here? A couple of weeks. But I've been at GenEx for a long time before."

"How long a time?"

"At least ten years. I was a kid when I came here."

"You were? Did they kidnap you, too? How'd they find out about what you could do?"

"My mom died. I kind of discovered what I could do at the youth group home I was sent to, by accident. A couple weeks after it happened, I was told I was being transferred to a new home, and I ended up here."

"Oh."

I think about it for a little while.

"Then how come you were put here after all this time?"

"I didn't like how things were going. I wanted to get out. I tried something, and it didn't work."

"What did you try?"

"I'm not discussing that with someone I don't know."

"I thought you said we had nothing better to do."

"Let's just say that once they've got you, you're with them for life."

"Well, that doesn't tell me anything."

"Drop it, kid."

My curiosity is making my tongue itch to ask more, but I swallow my questions. If living around a bunch of badly damaged people and having a past I don't like to discuss myself has taught me anything, it's to ignore the urge to ask.

"Fine, if you want to be that way about it. So, this place has been around for a long time, then?"

"It seemed to be pretty well established, when I first got here. From what I understand, they have offices in other parts of the world. I'm not entirely sure, though."

"How come I never heard of them before?"

"Well, they don't exactly advertise the whole 'we do experiments on people with superpowers' thing. I don't think they exactly want people to know about any of the things that they do."

"So what do they want, exactly? Why are they doing this?"

"I'm not sure. They're experimenting, but I don't know what they're trying to achieve. The one thing I know for sure, though, they don't want the public to find out about powers. I know they send people to take or warn people with special abilities on the outside all the time."

I guess that explains it. I've gotten a lot bolder with my powers, especially in the past couple of years. The rumors were bound to make their way outside of the strict context of the underworld. If they want to keep superpowers a secret, like she says, it's possible I've been a threat to their purpose, whatever that is.

"Well, that can't be the only thing they do."

"I told you, I don't know what they want. I'm not a mind-reader. I know it involves research, but what they do with the research is a mystery to me."

I sigh, and lean my head against the wall. I close my eyes, because the next question brings back painful and uncomfortable memories of the brothel, when I asked the same question of Luke back then, trapped in a cell not so very much unlike this one.

"So... what's going to happen to me?"

The question doesn't bring pain and uncomfortable silence on her part like it did Luke, at least.

"Well, they're gonna do some experiments on you, you know, CT scans, blood samples, all that stuff. Don't worry too much, it doesn't hurt. Then, they're gonna try to make you use your powers while monitoring your brain activity. That doesn't hurt, either."

"How long will it last?"

"Pretty much as long as it takes for them to get what they want. It depends on you."

I glare at the air vent, as if she could see me. I know she can't but it still feels good to do it anyway.

"Are you saying I should play nice and do what they say?"

"I'm saying unless you have a plan, the more you fight, the more difficult life will be for you. Trust me, I know all about it."

"Haven't you ever tried to escape?"

"Of course I have. Don't be stupid. They're too big and too well-organized, that's all. There's no escaping from them."

"I don't believe that. I'm sure there's a way. There's always a way. I've been in more desperate situations than this, I assure you."

"No, you haven't."

"You don't know me. I've dealt with big and well-organized, and I know what I can do."

"Sure, kid. But you don't know this place. I do. And I've tried. So no offense, but I'll believe it when I see it."

I click my tongue. I'm kind of annoyed at how easily she seems to have given up. Then again, as much as she doesn't know me, I don't know her, either, and I don't know what she's been through to be this hopeless.

"What about what he said, about letting you come and go as you please, once you prove your loyalty? How do you prove your loyalty? Couldn't you just get out and disappear once you're out?"

"Not exactly. They have psychics. That's how they make sure you won't do that. By making sure you have no intention of doing it."

"Oh."

That complicates matters. I've never had to deal with people who have superpowers before. But I've gotten out of stickier situations when I was barely aware of my own power, so I know I can do it.

"Well, I'll find a way."

"I hope so, kid. Take me with you if you do."

"Fine. Help me when the time comes and you've got yourself a deal."

"Sure."

She sounds completely unconvinced, but then, I can't blame her. She doesn't know me.

DATE AND TIME UNKNOWN - POSSIBLY DAY 4

It's two more days before someone comes to get me again. Meals are brought to me twice a day through a slot at the bottom of the door, but it's a real sophisticated kind of little door that I absolutely can't open from this side, and I never see a body part I can grab, so I haven't had any other opportunity to try anything yet. It's too bad; if I got to use my power on someone or something, I would be better now than ever before. I've never been so long without having a cigarette. I'm impressed with myself that I haven't burned everything combustible in this room. When the door opens this time, it's that gray-haired man who can cancel my power and the huge fuck that threw me across the room. The old man looks at me warily for a while, like he's wondering if I'm gonna do anything, and I am glad to see that his nose is swollen with a big purple bar across its bridge. When he sees I'm not trying anything, he seems to relax.

"You're to come with me."

He waits with an apprehensive look on his face, like he expects me to react badly, and I do take small pleasure in waiting until the point where the big guy takes a step toward me, probably to pick me up or drag me or something. Since I do have my dignity, I stand up, and make to follow them.

We walk outside into a hall that looks everything like a hospital, made of big cement blocks that are meant to look like bricks, painted an ugly shade of beige. The ceiling has the same fluorescent light that seems to never go off in my cell, and there seems to be a lot of doors on either side. I wonder if they're all cells like mine and Julie's; the spacing seems about right. Eventually, we cross into a larger hall, and we obviously arrive in a new area. This section has double doors, and they're much further apart. I wonder what kind of place they're going to take me to, and I try not to stress out about it. I need to keep my wits about me.

Surprisingly enough, the place they take me to seems to be one of them big communal showers like they have at public swimming pools. There's a plastic chair in there, and on it, a towel, a washcloth, a bar of soap, and blue scrubs. The gray-haired man gestures to it.

"You can have a shower. These are some spare clothes for you to wear."

I wait for them to turn around and give me some privacy, but of course, they don't. After all, I am a prisoner. It's not like I mind, exactly. I start to take off the ruins of my suit. Well, I do mind. But I sure as hell ain't going to let them know that. I strip completely, leaving what I took off in a pile on the floor. It's all burnt and useless now, anyway. That happens to me way too often. Maybe I really should start buying cheaper suits. I grab the soap and the washcloth, and take the quickest shower I ever have, even though I've been stewing in my juices for almost a week now.

I don't look at them as I wash, but I can feel their eyes on me, watching. I know this isn't a place like the brothel was, and they probably don't have those thoughts or intentions, but I can't help it. I haven't been naked in front of anyone except for Lori since those days, and it stings more than I'd like to admit to realize that I'm uncomfortable to the point of feeling sick, when I thought I was fine, and that was all behind me.

When I'm done, I pull on the blue scrubs, which are, strangely enough, exactly the right size, though there are no shoes, so I just put on my blackened leather ones, no socks. Only then do I untie my hair, comb it with my fingers, and redo my ponytail while walking toward them. The old man nods, and turns to lead us out into the hall again. We walk for some time before going into another room, which is already far less pleasant that the shower. There's a hospital bed in the middle of it, and all sorts of machines and devices all around it. I feel my heartbeat rising and I take a deep breath to push it down. Julie said this didn't hurt. We'll see if she was a liar.

It turns out she's not. They have me sit down, and a doctor comes in and examines me. I've never had a full physical before. It turns out I'm perfectly healthy, but it's still good to know. Next they take some blood samples, then bring me to a machine that looks like a giant tube, stick me inside, and have me hold still while they somehow take pictures of my brain. I try not to ask all the questions that are burning my tongue, and act as cooperative as my dignity will allow, biding my time until the next opportunity shows itself, but by the time they take me back to my cell, it still hasn't, and Harvey and the big man are still tailing my every step. I allow them to lock me back in. I have no appetite for the meal they leave with me, so I simply go to sit on my bed, ignoring it. The sheets and mattress were changed in my absence. Or maybe not; maybe this is a new cell. After all, I didn't really notice where I was when they took me out. I have to check.

"Julie? You still there?"

"Obviously. Where else am I gonna go?"

I find myself breathing a sigh of relief. Annoying as she can be, the simple presence of her voice has been a comfort I'm not sure I could do without.

"How long do you think they'll keep us in here?"

"Me? Indefinitely. You? Depends."

"Why?"

"Why what?"

I have to think of a way to ask that'll mean she has to answer both questions. I often get side-tracked from what I want to know in conversations because things come up that bring up more questions.

"Why is there a difference?"

That was a good one. She's quiet for a while, probably trying to figure out a way to answer.

"Well, they don't know you're a lost cause yet."

"So... does that mean you're a lost cause?"

"Yeah. I won't do what they want me to do."

"Why not?"

"I already told you, kid, I don't want to talk about it."

That's it. I've had about enough of this.

"If you don't stop calling me kid, I'm not gonna talk to you anymore."

I can almost hear her sigh.

"Fine, fine."

There is a pause until I remember what I wanted to know.

"So... if they don't keep me here so long, where will I go?"

"Depends. If you play nice, they'll probably transfer you to school."

"School?"

She starts laughing. I guess she must have heard the disgust in my voice. I never attended school past grade 6 or so. I was held back a year because I missed months of it at a time, the first time I escaped the house where I was born, and when I got away for good, I never had the time or the inclination to go back. It's not like I need it to do what I do.

"Yeah, school. Don't worry; it's not like regular school. Well, part of it is, I guess, like geography, and other things you need to know to do the things they want you to do. But mostly they teach you useful stuff. Like how to use your powers. And how to control them. It can be fun, if you let it."

Well. That doesn't sound so bad. And I'll get to actually meet others like me. If there really are others.

"Are there lots of people there?"

"At one time? Not so much. It's not exactly like we're a dime a dozen, you know. They have to look far to find us. But at one time, in a class, I've seen as many as ten. It's usually closer to five or six, though."

That gets my mind going. If there's anything my past experiences have taught me, it's that anything I can accomplish alone, I can do better with others there to help me. Maybe I'll find allies in there. Allies who aren't as jaded as Julie. People who haven't given up, yet. I'm so full of faith that this will work, it's even harder than usual to find sleep that night. If only I could have a cigarette.

DATE AND TIME UNKNOWN - POSSIBLY DAY 5

I run into the condo, looking around. There's the sweet smell of something cooking, something home-made, like Rosanna does, and everything looks bright, and clean, and happy somehow. I'm so glad I'm finally home.

"Lori? I'm home!"

I hear a high-pitched giggle, and I see Nicolas coming towards me. He seems excited, and I notice I'm holding his favorite toy, a squeaky plastic giraffe, and he's crawling, then standing and walking, his arms outstretched, his mouth stretched into a huge, toothless grin. I lean down to pick him up and hug him, but as I do, he's gone, and I'm left holding nothing but air. I look around, but there's no trace of him anywhere in the apartment. The light is gone, too, and the smell, and it just feels like something terrible is about to happen, so I start running, feeling a bit frantic. I get to the bathroom, and I see Lori hunched over the tub, her back to me. I start to sigh in relief, but something's wrong. She's too still. I walk to her carefully.

"Lori?"

She doesn't answer. I put my hand on her shoulder, trying to shake her to get her attention, but she just falls over. I don't need to check her; I can see by the needle in her arm and the stiffness of her body that she's dead. I take a step back, and notice there's something floating in the tub. I feel my entire body getting weak, except my stomach, which feels so tight and compressed I feel like I'm going to break in half. I can't look in there. I know what it is. I turn back to Lori, because it's easier to look at her than at him, and she's staring at me, her eyes all dead and sunken in, a cruel expression on her face.

"Where were you? We needed you!"

The sound of my own scream wakes me, and I calm down when I realize I've been dreaming. I scramble out of bed as soon as I remember I'm alone, and I'm not at home. How do I know this isn't happening right now? Or something even worse?

I run to the door to pound on it and scream again, but realize at the last minute how desperate that's going to make me seem, and I clench my fists and try to breathe, and then pace when that doesn't work. I hear Julie calling me again, asking if I'm ok, but my teeth are clamped so tight I wouldn't even know how to open my mouth if I wanted to. My heart's pumping like crazy, and no matter what I try, I can't seem to calm down. I need a cigarette so bad I could chew my fingers off if it would make the need go away. How long have I been in here? It's only been a few days, by my count, but I could be wrong. It feels like forever. And who knows how long I was out before I woke up? What's Lori doing? Would she have the good sense to go to Luke for help? Would Luke come by, and stay to help, when he realized

I was missing? Would Lupino take Nicolas, if he suspected something was wrong? I can't wait until I get out of here anymore. It's been too long already. What will be there waiting for me when I return? Julie's still calling me.

"Alex?"

"What?"

I take another deep breath as she answers me. That was a lot more aggressive than I meant it to be, but she doesn't seem deterred when she talks to me again.

"Are you ok?"

"I'm fine. Why?"

"Because you're making it way too hot again. And you were screaming."

I sigh, and sit with my head in my hands, breathing, concentrating, until she talks again.

"That's better. So what's up?"

I grit my teeth, trying to keep from getting angry again. It's not something I have a lot of practice with.

"I'm fine. All right?"

"You're a liar."

I walk right up to the wall and punch it, bruising my knuckles on the unbreakable ceramic. What is the matter with this girl?

"So what? Who cares?"

"Well, obviously, I do."

"You don't even know me!"

"No, but I have nothing else to do. So why don't you talk to me?"

I sigh and sit on the bed again, leaning my back against the wall.

"I just... There's people outside that depend on me. I don't know how they're doing without me."

"Where do they think you are?"

"I don't know. They probably don't know, either."

"What do you mean?"

"They just took me. They grabbed me from the streets, and nobody knows where I am."

"Really?"

"Yeah."

"That's weird."

I frown.

"Why weird? Didn't you say they did that?"

"Well, in a way, yes... but mostly they had ways of making people go, like prison, or some kind of health institute, or something. You know, legal means. I never heard of them just grabbing someone off the streets like that. That would just be stupid."

"Stupid how?"

"Well... then people would come looking, right? Authorities would be alerted... that's my understanding of it, anyway."

I bring up my knees to hug them, and lean my chin on my arms, thinking. Has someone alerted the authorities? I know I don't have a good relationship with the law, but... well, if someone asked, they would have to look for me... wouldn't they? I have no idea.

"Alex?"

"What?"

"Well, you just got all quiet. What's on your mind?"

"Nothing. A lot. It's complicated."

"Hah! I got time for complicated."

I pick at some lint on my blue scrubs and think about it. I've never really talked to someone about that kind of stuff. But now... it's true there's nothing else to do. Somehow, not being able to see her, it feels like it might be easier. And maybe, in return, I might get some more answers about this place.

I'm about to open my mouth when the door swings open, and I spring to my feet. Harvey walks in, looking down at his notepad like I'm not even there. He stands there, reading in my face, and I feel my fists clenching so hard my nails bite into my skin, and that's saying something, because lately I've been biting them until they bleed. I manage to breathe, though, because there's no use in getting mad, not with him, not when I can't use my power. He finally looks up at me.

"You're to follow me, mister Winters."

Fantasizing very vividly about ripping the metal toilet off the wall and bashing his skull in with it, I walk to him slowly, somehow managing to keep my calm. Well, on the outside, anyway. He turns his back on me and leads me out of the room. I hope for a minute, but when I walk out I spy the huge dude hanging back, waiting for me to try something. I don't. They take me down the hall to a carpeted section of the building I've never been in. We take a couple steps, and he veers off into an office, opening the door and motioning me to step inside. I frown, walk in slowly, and the rage hits me like a wall. Greasy Snake Finley is sitting at a desk, looking over some papers. I grit my teeth, and concentrate on clenching and unclenching my fists. Harvey stands at the back of the room, acting like he's not really there. Finley eventually looks up at me, and motions for a seat across his desk, smiling his snake smile.

"Mister Winters! Please! Have a seat."

"I'll stand."

He shrugs.

"Suit yourself. I have the results of your tests, here. Your control of your abilities is, as expected, impressive."

I say nothing. I try to keep my face as neutral as possible, which is pretty hard to do, when all I want to do is rip off his head and spit down his throat. He frowns at something that's written in his file.

"It does seem you have neglected your health, though. It is good we caught you at such a young age. Your blood pressure is elevated. You should learn to manage your stress better."

I grit my teeth so hard I think I might actually chip them. If I jumped over the desk, right now, would I have time to beat this guy to death before the big dude walked in? Would they let me go, afterward? I breathe through my nose and remind myself why I'm playing nice. I think of Nicolas, and Lori. They need me.

He smiles at me again, this time he looks amused. I have never wanted to punch someone as badly as I do this guy, right now.

"It would seem you've decided to cooperate. I cannot express how glad I am to see this. I think you will be very happy here."

I can't hold it in anymore. I have to do something, even if that's just talking.

"Happy? How the hell long do you think you'll keep me here, anyway?"

He shrugs looking mildly put out, like I'm not even saying anything worth hearing.

"Indefinitely, I would think. It will be some time before we are sure enough of you to begin your education, and then that will certainly take several months, if not years. By that time, you will surely be ready to accept the fact that you are working for us."

"What about my family, huh? Or my friends? Don't you think they'll be looking for me? You can't just keep me here."

He has the gall to chuckle, shaking his head like I'm cute.

"What makes you think I can't?"

I'm feeling doubtful, suddenly. But Julie said they didn't do that. And I have to know, at least, what they think. Where the people that care about me think I am.

"Well... it's illegal. I mean, if you're a professional kidnapper, you're gonna get caught, eventually, no?"

He outright laughs, this time. I clench my fists so hard I think the bones in my fingers might snap.

"Surely, you are not telling me that one cannot lead a life of crime without being caught? You of all people should know that isn't true!"

I wait for him to go on. I hate being laughed at, especially when I feel like I'm missing the joke. His laughter eventually quiets, and he shrugs.

"Besides, we are not professional kidnappers. We help people with abilities. A lot of them come willingly. You, well... you are a special case."

"What are you talking about?"

He grins at me and opens his file again, looking down at it.

"On paper, Alex Winters was reported missing by his parents when he ran away at thirteen years of age. He hasn't been heard of since. Surely you would know this. You could be dead, and if no one found your body, no one would open an investigation into your disappearance. You were considered a closed case many years ago. The police don't normally reopen investigations that old."

I try to keep my face neutral, but I can feel my knees going weak. I want nothing more than to sit down right now, like all the strength's been drained out of me. I'd never really thought about the repercussions of having no paper trail for so long. Everything I have as an I.D. – certificates, learner's permit, everything – is a high quality fake. I always thought it would make me harder to identify, or trace, if I ever got caught, but I never imagine it would play against me. I somehow manage to stay standing, though I think Finley must see the defeat in my eyes, because he has a grin I don't like, and just nods to Harvey, who leads me back outside. I follow him down the hall, dazed, back to the area where they run experiments. I'm on my own. I guess I knew that already, at least a little. I've never really been on my own before; I always had Jimmy, or Luke, or even mister Lupino, to help me decide what to do. I have no idea if I'm capable of coming up with a plan and making it happen on my own. I guess we'll find out.

It's easier than it's ever been to play nice for the rest of the day. Right now, I feel like all the fight's gone out of me.

DATE AND TIME UNKNOWN – PROBABLY DAY 9

The door opening rips all my power to concentrate away from me. I've been jonesing so bad for a smoke lately, it's real hard not to snap at everyone that I see or hear, even Julie. Added to the fact that I've had to stuff every shred of dignity down to the bottom of my being so I can play nice and hope to be transferred to that stupid school thing, and cranky doesn't even begin to define the mood I'm in. It hasn't helped that Julie has consistently been making fun of me and my plan, telling me it's never gonna work. Funny thing is, she's made me promise a second and third time that if it does work, I'll come back for her, so somewhere, she must have some faith in me. I hope.

It's Harvey the gray-haired man at the door again, and my hopes fall. Every time it's him, he just takes me to that stupid room where I have to use my power to make things warm or cool, or burn them as a machine measures whatever the hell my brain is doing through electrodes stuck all over my head. Looks like it's gonna be more of that today. I follow him docilely, pushing down thoughts of jumping him and strangling him. I've been having them ever since the big man stopped escorting him, a couple days ago, but harboring

115

these fantasies make it hard to show a good face when I need to, which is pretty much all the time. I'm so concentrated that I don't notice we're not headed the same way we usually are until we're all the way down another hall. There are windows in here, on either side, and I can see it's a walkway that connects two separate buildings. There's forest on either side, as far as I can see; so this place isn't in town like I thought it was. At least, that's something to go on. I'll know to take some survival stuff with me when I break out of this place.

We pass through one last set of heavy, double doors, and the hall we walk into when we reach the other building already looks a lot less like a hospital than the place we just left. The walls are yellow, and though there are a series of secure, electronically-locked doors on one side, we also pass a set of double doors with windows through which I see what looks like an old-fashioned gym, just like the one we had at school, when I was growing up. My heart jumps. Could this be the school Julie was talking about? Did I make it? Did I finally win their trust? I have a small pang of regret when I finally realize that I've made it. For all her attitude, I'm gonna miss Julie. I swear I'll get her out if I can, though.

Gray Harvey takes me, quiet as always, to a place that looks like a dorm room, with a single bed on either side, a small dresser next to each, and two desks and chairs. There's no one there, but one side is obviously occupied, since there are a bunch of the same blue scrubs I'm wearing on the floor, and the bed is unmade.

"This is your room. You will find spare clothes in the drawers of your dresser. You are free to come and go around the school during daytime hours, but after curfew, at seven, you must remain in your room."

I'm so excited not only to have what I want, but to hear that I can go around as I please, that I almost forget to play dumb.

"School?"

"Yes. You will be attending our school from now on. The other students are having lunch as we speak. Follow me."

I follow him back out, and he takes me further into the hall, past a few more doors just like the one that leads to my new room, and one or two that appear to be leading to traditional looking classrooms, until we reach an open area that looks exactly like the cafeteria we had in elementary school, but on a much smaller scale. There are only three tables that could all in all sit a maximum of thirty people, and an open area in the wall at the bottom of the room where there is a counter with warmers, and food that I can't distinguish yet. There are seven people sitting, split up in one large group, and a smaller one. They're all eyeing me, some defiantly, some inquisitively, some so shyly they barely look up. Gray Harvey takes me to the counter, hands me a tray and utensils, and walks away. I take a look at the food as a lady dressed in white gives me an annoyed sigh, like it's my fault I've come in late, and serves me a plate. There's some kind of indescribable meat in gravy, mashed potatoes, and cooked frozen peas. I've had worse. She hands me a glass of water and a tiny carton of milk, and as I turn back towards the sitting area, I'm having flashbacks of school, and cliques, and trying to find your place in one when you're a sour kid with a temper.

The largest group seems to be sizing me up. I can immediately tell which one's the leader; he's tall and big, and grins at me with a cocksure air that rubs me the wrong way. But if I'm going to get myself the maximum number of allies, I gotta make friends with everyone, and I know enough about school dynamics to know that starts with the largest group. I head that way.

Apart from the large guy, there's a smaller guy who jitters like he can't stop himself from constantly moving and a short, skinny bleached blonde girl with dark roots, who I'm sure would have been covered in an inch of makeup and dyed her hair even blonder if she'd had the opportunity. She's tied the top of her scrubs and pulled down her pants as low as they'll go on her hips so we can see her navel. The last girl, a plump but pretty Latina, has thick, naturally curly brown hair, and enough self-confidence to understand that fashion doesn't mean much if we're all wearing the same thing. I set my tray next to the jittery guy, and he giggles nervously in a high, grating voice. It's the big one that speaks, though, as I'm sitting down.

"Someone say you could sit here, fag?"

I raise an eyebrow, but my face remains neutral. So, he's one of those. He looks about my age; I guess it's people like that that make others call me kid. I'd probably feel the same if everyone I knew of my age was this immature. I don't say anything; we'll see what he makes of me. I've faced down people who had the real and pressing intention of killing me in a variety of painful ways; no amount of jock is ever going to impress me. The blonde girl and the jittery guy look between me and him nervously, like they're expecting a confrontation, which unfortunately, does seem inevitable, but the Latina girl is smiling at me like she thinks I'm interesting. The large guy looks around at his posse, nervously. He's obviously not used to leaving people unimpressed, and he's feeling threatened. He has to find a way to reaffirm his dominance, quick.

"This table's for people with cool powers. You got a cool power?"

I smirk, but I'm careful not to let it touch my eyes. I've had that expression turned on me often enough to know how psychotic it can make you look, and I need to impress on this guy that I mean business.

"Well. Yes and no."

He frowns stupidly, and I can see in that moment how much of his brainpower is pure testosterone.

"What do you mean, yes and no?"

"It depends what you mean by cool."

I open my hand, palm up, and make a ball of fire that flashes large and high for a fraction of a second, before settling into an apple-sized flame in my hand. It has the desired effect; everyone jumps back for a moment, and the Latina girl laughs.

"Awesome!"

The leader guy looks at the positive reaction of his group, and like any leader who's at least good enough to stay in charge, goes with the impression of the moment.

"Fine. You can sit down here. What's your name?"

"I'm Alex."

"I'm Russell. This is Norman, but we call him Speedy."

I nod at the guy as he introduces him. I can see why he's called that. The guy looks like he just drank eight cans of Red Bull. He points to the blonde girl afterwards, and last to the Latina.

"This is Jill, and that's Naomi."

I nod, and glance at the other three sitting by themselves at another table. This is a good opportunity to gauge the level of hostility between the two.

"What about your friends over there?"

"Oh, they're not our friends. They're fags."

I resist the urge to roll my eyes, and simply raise an eyebrow at him. I understand how the dynamic works, though. A lot of people have no means of showing their strength without putting down others, and I guess fag is his go-to bad word. He probably lacks the imagination to think of other words, or to realize that it's not even an insult. It seems like I've got my work cut out for me. Russell ignores my expression, watching the three guys at the other table. I shake my head slightly and start eating my food. It tastes like wet cardboard, but it's no different than the food they've been feeding me under the door for the week and a half I've been here, and not much worse than the TV dinners I used to buy for me and Lori. I have a painful pressure on my chest at the thought of Lori, and especially Nicolas, wondering how they're doing. I gotta work fast to get out of here. They need me.

"So tell me. Any of you guys have cigarettes?"

They look at each other, and Naomi sighs wistfully.

"I wish. Don't think I haven't tried. There's no way to get any."

I sigh and rub my face. It was worth a try. I'm starting to get used to it a little, but it's hard to concentrate without being able to smoke.

"So, uh, how long have you guys been here?"

Russell shrugs.

"Me, I've been here almost a year. I was one of the first to get here, but there were other people when I came. They're gone now."

"Gone where?"

"They got jobs. I've seen them around. I'm almost done with my training. Then, I can have a job too."

"What kind of jobs?"

"I dunno. Guarding, bringing people like us here, I guess."

That gives me a window to ask. I gotta be careful how I phrase things, though.

"So... how did you get here?"

"Got in a huge car crash. But I didn't have a scratch on me. That's how I found out I was invincible. Then, a couple guys came to tell me there was a place where I could learn to do better with my powers, and learn how to be, like, a superhero. So I came here."

Damn. I should have known not everyone would be here against their will.

"So... you're happy here? It doesn't bother you that you can't leave?"

He shrugs.

"Where would I go? Besides, when they give me a job, I'll be able to come and go like I want. It's not that bad."

Speedy leans in to share; he speaks real fast, and when he does, he bounces on his chair with the rhythm of his words.

"Me, I wanna go. They tell me I'm unstable. I'm not unstable. Just everything is too slow here. Much too slow. I wanna run. I like running. But they tell me I can't run. I can't go. I wanna go. It's not fair. Why can't I go?"

Russell raises a hand, as if to stop him.

"All right, Speedy, shut up, we get it."

I turn to the girls.

"What about you?"

Naomi shrugs with one shoulder, drinking her water.

"Hey, it was this or juvie, for me, so it's not so bad. I don't say I wouldn't rather be back home, but it could be worse."

Jill rubs her elbow uncomfortably, staring at her plate, not answering. I'm about to press the issue, but just then Harvey comes into the cafeteria and points to a clock on the wall. Speedy springs from his seat like a jack-in-the-box, and flies to the front of the room literally faster than I can see. I guess his demeanor is not the only thing he gets his name from. Once he gets close to Harvey, he slows down dramatically, though he's no less excited when he stands. I guess Harvey's power has that kind of effect on everyone, not just me.

Everyone else starts to get up, and bring their trays back to the counter, so I do like the others. The next part is the difficult one for me, as they all line up in a rank with their hands clasped behind their back like soldiers, but I told myself I was going to be the cooperative little student they wanted me to be, so I do it anyway. After looking them over nonchalantly and nodding once, Harvey leads them out, and I follow them as they exit the cafeteria and make their way all the way down the hall and through an open door, leading us to an honest-to-goodness classroom, with a whiteboard and these funny little seats that have a half-desk attached to the chair on the right side. There's paper and pencils on the desk portions, and everyone grabs a seat in what looks like a status-oriented order that they've quietly defined as a group. I never got to that part of school; in elementary, everything was alphabetical, and I was always the last one on the list, so I sit in the back like I'm used to. Besides, with his broken nose, I doubt Harvey wants me right in his face. He does seem to be more watchful around me. When everyone's seated, he turns to the board, and I have to refrain from laughing when I realize I beat up a math teacher. It doesn't last, though. It's five minutes before I realize I have no idea what this guy is talking about. Since when does math have letters instead of numbers? And we're supposed to find out what numbers the letters represent? What does that even mean? Are they seriously expecting me to sit through this without smoking?

I quickly lose interest, and start doodling on the paper on my desk. I guess I'm too far behind to catch up, but I don't feel bad about it at all. I mean, letters that represent hidden numbers? When's that ever gonna be useful in real life? I know when an earner is holding back on his payment, and that's all the math I need in my life. Harvey notices what I'm doing, but I give him a stare and he doesn't call me out on it. After math comes geography, and I'm reminded of why I thought Mikov's brothel was not so bad after all. There is a clock above the white board, and I swear the hand that marks the seconds only ticks every minute. This is hell. I died and I've gone to hell. There's no other explanation.

PROBABLY DAY 9, 6:17 PM

That stupid school business took so much out of me I didn't have the energy to work on questioning the others at dinner. I don't know how long I'm gonna last in this place; I'm starting to feel real pressure to get the hell out of here, and quick. I hate that I still have no idea how I'm gonna do it. It means I've still got a long way to go.

When we're sent back to our rooms for the curfew, it seems I'm rooming with one of the guys from the other table, a short dude with a mushroom cut that can't be older than fourteen or so. He goes to his side of the room, and watches me while I take inventory of everything there is on my side of the room. Seeing as that's only a desk, a chair, a bed, a dresser and a couple changes of blue scrubs, it doesn't take me long, and all we've got left to do is stare at each other. He's sitting on his bed, hugging his knees, watching me like he doesn't know what to make of me.

"Hey. I'm Alex."

"I'm Clay. Hi."

I lie down on my back on the bed. I don't think this kid can help me escape, and frankly, I'm too wiped out right now to try and find out. I think of Nicolas again. What if I'm stuck here forever? What if he grows up without a dad? With Lori as a mom? The kid on the other bed clears his throat.

"Hey... I know you're worried, and you seem like a nice guy... so I thought I'd warn you."

I frown at him. What the hell is he talking about?

"What?"

"Your thoughts. I know you want to see your boy again, but... you should try not to think about escaping."

I sit up, frowning at him. How does this guy know all this?

"Ok. Explain. Now."

"Your thoughts. I can hear them. You're a pretty intense guy."

He seems uncomfortable, so I suppose he's not really doing it on purpose.

"So. You're a mind-reader, then?"

He nods, relaxing. I guess he must be used to people getting pretty pissed off when he reads their mind.

"Yeah."

"What did you mean about warning me? Warning me against what? You?"

He shakes his head enthusiastically.

"Oh, no. Against the others."

"What others?"

"The other psychics. They do random checks. Loyalty checks. And when you've got a strong personality, well... you project a lot more."

"Project?"

"You know... Your thoughts. They're loud."

"Oh."

I think about it. I've never really had to worry about what I was thinking before. How do I control that, on top of everything else I gotta worry about?

"I could... I could help you, you know."

I look up at him. This really does take some getting used to, thinking something, and having someone hear you.

"Help me how?"

"Well... I can shield your thoughts, for starters."

I squint at him. I don't trust people easily, and it's especially hard for me to believe anyone would offer me something for free. There's always a string attached.

"Why would you do that?"

He shrugs.

"Why not? You seem like someone nice. I could hear you really didn't agree with what Russell was saying. And I understand why you have to hang out with him. I don't want to see anything bad happen to you."

I'm still not convinced.

"And in exchange?"

"Maybe you could... stand up for us? And if you do make it out of this place..."

"Yeah, yeah, I know. Take you with me."

He has a small smile.

"I wish I could be more help. But I'm not that strong, and I'm not that brave."

"Hey, you're helping by keeping me out of trouble, right? That makes you all right in my book. So, do I have to do anything special to help you shield me, or anything?"

"Not really. Just remember that I'm only able to keep it up as long as I'm awake, and as long as you're in the same room with me. If I lose sight of you, you're on your own. Sorry."

"Don't worry, it's good enough. Better than what I can do, anyway. So how did you get here?"

He looks uncomfortable again, like the memory pains him, and he shrugs.

"My parents. They knew about what I could do. Maybe it would have helped if I had shut up about it. Anyway, they did some research. This place passes itself off as a school for people with special abilities, a place that 'helps' people like me." He mimics quotation marks with his fingers when he says the word 'helps'. "So they sent me here. I think they were just glad to be rid of me, to tell you the truth. They haven't visited, called or even written since I came here. I tell myself that it's because this place is more like a concentration camp than a school, but..." He sighs. "Other people have gotten letters. Jill still writes her parents. As long as she doesn't say anything weird or whatever, she's allowed to get letters and send them."

"Huh."

Maybe if I ask, they'd let me send some letters too. Explain to everyone that I haven't abandoned them. That I'm coming back for them.

"They read what you write, you know. There's a lot of things you're not allowed to say."

I look up at him.

129

"Are you just going to read every single thought I have?"

"I can't help it, you know. I'm kind of in your head, putting up the shield there. Everything you think is like background noise, it's actually kind of an effort to keep it out."

I shrug. If it can't be helped, it can't be helped. I'd rather have the shield than my privacy, at this point.

"All right. So long as you don't go telling everyone what you hear, I'm fine with it."

"You don't have anything to worry about from me."

PROBABLY DAY 10, 7:09 AM

Clay waits for me at the room door while I finish pulling on the pants to my scrubs. It's way too early to be up. What is wrong with these people? How can I even have breakfast this early? Who gets up before ten, anyway? Does anything at all ever happen before ten? I know Mister Lupino does it, but I mean, he's old, and I only have to meet him this early on really, really rare occasions. They can't seriously be expecting me to get up at this time every day. And these stupid scrubs. I've worn tailor-made Italian suits since I was fifteen years old, and nothing else. Now I feel like I have to walk around in my pajamas all day and I just hate it. I run my hands through my hair to comb it and redo my ponytail as I walk to the door.

"Stupid scrubs. Why don't they give us real clothes?"

He shrugs.

"I really don't know. Maybe it's a budget thing."

I snort. I don't care what it is. Even if I wasn't stressing out about everything that is probably falling apart

131

without me on the outside, I am so sick of this place if I only had the opportunity I would burn it to bits. He turns the handle and walks out, and for a second, I'm taken aback.

"The door is always unlocked?"

"Well, yeah. Or else we couldn't get inside."

We start the short walk to the cafeteria.

"But then... we could just walk out?"

He shakes his head.

"There's surveillance cameras in the halls to make sure you respect curfew. And the doors that would lead out of this part of the building have these really complicated electronic locks on them."

I raise an eyebrow at him.

"How do you know all this?"

"That weird guy, that sits with the others? The one they call Speedy? He tried escaping once."

"Oh. So, I guess that didn't work, did it."

He just shakes his head as we walk into the cafeteria.

"No way. They caught him before he broke through the door. They dragged him back kicking and screaming."

We grab some trays from the end of the counter, and I wait for him to continue his story.

"All the guards here are just like us. In fact, when we get out of this place, that's what they'll have us do."

"How do you know all that?"

He gives me a withering look, and I remember that he can read thoughts.

"Oh. Right."

He sighs.

"When I first got here, there was another guy in the group. He graduated, though. Now he patrols the halls at night, with a gun, and he keeps us in."

I frown as the lady behind the counter hands me a bowl of oatmeal that looks more like gray sludge. It's just like Russell said, and I remember Julie discussing something like that, and even that snake Finley, too. So eventually I'll graduate to being a guard. How long until I get to go out? There is absolutely no way that I am waiting that long. Even if people didn't depend on me, I don't want to miss Nicolas growing up. We turn back to the tables, and Clay sort of stands there, looking at me, as if wondering where I'm going to go. The two people in his group are looking at me curiously, as are the others; the only one that doesn't seem to care where I sit, or that I'm there at all, is Russell. He's looking at his oatmeal and eating it like he hasn't got a care in the world, but I can tell by the stiffness in his shoulders and his jaw that he's really tense. I shrug at Clay, and he gives me a small nod to say that he understands, and we go our separate ways. I've all but won the smaller group by befriending Clay. These four are going to be the harder ones, so I need to keep working at it if I want all the allies I can get.

Russell glares at me when I sit down, and it's all I can do not to laugh when I realize he's trying to give me the cold look that Jimmy has when he's threatening someone. I must have made an impression, yesterday.

"What the hell were you doing talking to that fag?"

I shake my head.

"He's my roommate. So what?"

"So, are you a fag?"

I've had enough of this. I almost groan with the annoyance, and I roll my eyes at him.

"Give it a fucking rest, Russell. Even if I was, I could still beat the shit out of you, and then what would that make you?"

He puts his spoon down and gives me that look again like he's trying to be scary.

"What did you say?"

I give him my coldest look, and pick up my juice box – a freakin' juice box – to drink from it.

"You heard me."

He stands, swiping my tray and throwing it to the floor. I watch him calmly, not flinching. I was expecting this. This is where we make our stand; I'm tired of his bullshit, and he's too insecure to have me in his group without having to assert his semblance of authority over me. He's so pissed off his face is red, but I can tell he's hesitating. One thing I've learned over the years is you can see it in someone's eyes when they mean business, especially if you've ever been in a real fight before. I'm more business than most people can handle, and I'm not scared of this punk. He doesn't have time to make up his mind, because Naomi puts her hand on his forearm.

"Don't start something, Russell. You don't want to get in trouble."

He glares at her, and stalks off, leaving the cafeteria, putting a swagger in his step like leaving is actually what he intended to do all along. I watch him go, and pull his breakfast toward me, eating it. Jill and Speedy are looking between me and the door nervously, and Naomi just sort of watches me, her lips pursed. I finish Russell's gruel, and then push the plate away, looking at her.

"What?"

She shrugs.

"You know this isn't over, right? I wouldn't underestimate Russell. He's pretty strong, and hard to beat, even with that fire of yours. You know he's invincible, right?"

I smile a bit.

"I've seen invincible. I've seen immortal. I'm not impressed."

I've killed people with my power. Not just people. Freaky vampires with super strength and speed, too. I know what his power is, and I don't care; I can take him. She seems to watch me as though she's making up her mind, and then shrugs.

"I guess we'll see soon enough."

PROBABLY DAY 10, 10:42 AM

This is so much better than what we did yesterday. Jill's disappeared into the floor, but I'm waiting for her. As soon as she comes out again, I'll have her, this time. I heat up the entire area where she was at, enough to feel, but not enough to burn. Those are the instructions; we're supposed to fight, but not to bring real hurt to each other. At least not on purpose.

As it turns out, every morning is spent in the gym. It's a big, open area, that looks a lot more modern than the forty-year old monkey bars and wooden benches they had at the school I went to. It's all painted white, with fresh paint and everything. The guy teaching us is like a freaking drill sergeant, but I like him better than Harvey. At least, he's straightforward. At first, it was like a normal gym class, where we ran and did push-ups and sit-ups and all sorts of other exercises, but then it turned into something indescribably cool where we had to fight each other using our powers. Well, it was cool for me. I started out against Jill. It turns out she can become intangible, like a ghost. She can disappear through walls, and my fire goes right through her. It's a pretty cool power to have, though it seems to me it's real defensive. She reappears behind me and taps me on the shoulder.

"Boom. I've killed you. Again. I guess fire's not that great."

"Where'd you come from?"

"I traveled through the floor, of course."

"And what do you mean, I'm dead?"

She raises her eyebrows like she can't believe how stupid I am.

"Do I need to spell it out for you? I can phase through anything. That includes your skull."

She waves her fingers at me, and I suddenly have the image of this small girl with her hand inside the back of my head, squeezing my brain.

"Eww."

She giggles. I haven't known her for that long, true, but I get the feeling she's not usually this happy. It's amazing what showing off what you do best can do to some people.

"So how come you're still here, then?"

She frowns.

"What do you mean?"

"Well, if you can walk through walls, and doors, how come you haven't left?"

She shrugs, looking suddenly shy and uncomfortable again.

"It's not so bad here. Besides, they're teaching us stuff about our powers. And..."

"Ow! Stop!"

I whip my head around. That was Clay. He was pitted against Russell this morning, which seems kind of unfair, but I know better than most people that situations you encounter in real life are almost never fair. I didn't expect what I'm seeing, though. Russell's holding him by the collar, and beating the crap out of him. Clay has his arms up to defend himself, though that doesn't seem to do much at all. The drill sergeant is watching, but doing nothing, though he clearly said we weren't supposed to really hurt each other. I run to Russell, grab him by the back of the shirt, and pull him off Clay with every ounce of strength I have. I'm surprised at how easy it is; I've not only grown bigger in the last year, I've gotten stronger, too.

He gets up and glares at me. I stare right back, concentrating, covering my hands with flame, more for the effect than any real purpose.

"Think about it. You really wanna take me on?"

The sergeant is watching us to see what'll happen, and I can see Russell hesitate. He's not completely sure he wants to take me on yet, but he takes one look at the others and he knows that if he backs down this time, he's not

139

in charge anymore. He raises his fists, and lunges at me. I'm sure he thinks he's taking me by surprise, but he's slow, and this is far from being the first fight I've ever been in. I take a step back, letting him think I'm scared, but at the last minute, I step aside and trip him in the same movement. He stumbles forward, but doesn't fall. I can see from the corner of my eye that all the others are scrambling away from our fight, though I keep my attention on him. Once the coast is clear, I send him a blast of fire as he turns around. He raises his arms protectively. I don't hold back, but he's not even screaming. This is going to be harder than I thought, but he's gotta have a weakness. I'm not going to waste any time hitting him if even my fire can't hurt him, but I might have an idea, if I can make it work. I see him advancing again, through the fire, though he's going slowly, since he can't really see. Once he's close, I dodge him again, this time kicking him on the back of the knee, breaking his stride and sending him sprawling to the floor.

I don't lose a single second; he's taller than me, so it works out to my advantage. I jump on his back, lock my legs around his waist, and clamp my hands over his nose and mouth. He starts thrashing around, trying to get me off his back, and by the way he panics, I figure my little stunt is working. That's good, because I don't know how long I'll be able to hold on. He tries to pull me off by my clothes, but to my surprise, I'm as strong as he is. He manages to grab my ponytail and yanks hard. It hurts, but I've been hurt a lot worse, many, many times, and I'm able to concentrate on my grip on his face and forget about it. He lets himself fall on his back, thinking to crush me, but I see it coming and brace myself, so the shock is not too bad; it doesn't even crack a single rib, and I've had my ribs broken often enough to know. He keeps trying to crush me, and I admit it's a little harder to breathe, but I can feel him weakening, so I hold on. His movements get more sluggish, until he's practically passed out; and it's only then that the instructor steps forward.

"That's enough. Let him go."

I consider holding on just because he's telling me to let go, but I don't really want to kill him, and I don't want to get put back into that cell, either. I release him, and he rolls off of me, gasping for air. I get up and dust myself off. The instructor is giving me a look I can't read, and just when I think he's going to bite my head off, he nods once.

"Well done. No one's taken him down before."

I nod and try not to smile. I don't want to please this guy; I don't want to please any of them, but I've gotten little enough praise in my life that it takes me by surprise every time. Russell gets up and glares at me, and he looks like he's going to start something, but the instructor steps between us and looks at him.

"Take a break, Russell."

He glares at me one last time, and walks off to sit on one of the benches next to the wall. I stare at him as he goes, and then turn to look at Clay. Naomi's holding a handkerchief to his nose, which is bleeding pretty bad. I kneel next to him, looking him over. I've never studied first aid or anything, but I've been seriously injured enough times to be able to tell when someone else is. He doesn't seem to have anything broken. Well, maybe his nose.

"You ok?"

He nods, taking the handkerchief from Naomi's hand. I look at the drill-sergeant-gym-teacher pointedly, and he rolls his eyes.

"What?"

"He needs to have this looked after. Probably even set. I suppose you have an infirmary?"

"Yeah, fine. Clay, go to the infirmary."

I think about what he told me last night, and remember that I'm better off being in the same room as him.

"I'll take him. Anyway, you need an even number to pair us off, no?"

The guy looks at Clay, and sighs, nodding.

"Fine. Jill, you're with Russell. Everyone else, there's nothing more to see. Resume."

They get back to their confrontations as I help Clay stand and walk out of the gym. Once we're out in the hall, he detaches from me, walking by himself, still holding the bloody handkerchief against his nose.

"Danks, ban."

I chuckle.

"Hey, sure. So, do you know where the infirmary is?"

He points down the hall, close to the entrance I came in through. We start walking.

"So, what was Russell's problem, anyway?"

He takes away the handkerchief, and sniffs a bit, immediately making a grossed-out face, but it doesn't look like he's bleeding anymore, and when he talks, he doesn't seem so congested.

"He called me a fag. Again. I pointed out that since I can read thoughts, it might be a good idea to pick a different insult, since I knew the reason why he used it all the time."

I lift an eyebrow, amused and interested. It makes sense; I should have known. Clay rolls his eyes.

"Oh yeah, he's really insecure about his sexuality. It's kind of pathetic."

I laugh. Clay chuckles too, and his nose starts bleeding again. He curses and blots it up.

As we near the entrance to the building, I can see that one of the high-security doors on the right side of the wall is ajar, and it piques my curiosity. Before I can take a look inside, a door on the other side of the hall opens, and Clay stops dead in his tracks, his whole body stiffening. I stop too, and watch him for a short while, until I notice his eyes are wide and fixed on the door that just opened.

A wheelchair comes through, pushed by someone who looks like a nurse. There's a young guy in it, younger than Clay, even, maybe twelve or thirteen, hooked up to a couple of IVs. His head hangs oddly, a bit to the side, with his mouth open, like he's some kind of vegetable. I've seen people like that at the hospital before, usually stroke victims, unable to move a muscle or make a single expression. I wonder if that's what happened to this guy, and what he's doing here if it is. Then I think that maybe some experiment went wrong, and I have to get out of this place before something like that happens to me. And then, something real strange happens.

The guy doesn't move a single muscle, but his eyes swivel in his head, suddenly focusing on me, and the look in them is intense, like I've seen few people able to pull off before, and I have the distinct impression he wants to say something. They hold me for a few seconds, and then they turn to give Clay the same look. The whole thing lasts just a few seconds, and then the guy is wheeled in through the open security door, which closes behind him. I'm about to comment on how weird that was, when Clay suddenly grabs my arm. I look at him. He's pale, and breathing kind of hard.

"Hey, you ok?"

He nods, and I simultaneously hear his voice in my head, telling me we'll discuss it later, and in my ears, saying, "Yeah, I'm just light-headed from the blood loss." I'm about to tell him how freaky that is, but then I remember that since I thought it, he probably heard it, and he gives me a small nod to confirm that he did. I don't know if I'm ever going to get used to this.

PROBABLY DAY 10, 6:02 PM

I close the door to our room, and I'm finally alone with Clay in a place where we can talk. Knowing that there was something to discuss secretly has made the whole day go by so much slower than yesterday, which is saying something. I wanted to spend the entire day just screaming. I think I finally know what it means to feel like a teenager.

"All right. We're alone, and we can talk. Wanna tell me what happened in the hall today, with that weird dude?"

Clay looks at the door nervously, like we're in some danger. I can't imagine what's a more delicate subject than escaping around here, but it does seem to make him real nervous, 'cause his voice is a whisper.

"He spoke to me. In my mind."

I raise an eyebrow. I suspected as much; so that guy really wasn't brain-dead.

"No, of course he wasn't brain-dead! I've heard him before, too. He's tried to make contact before, but I never

145

knew where he was, or what he really wanted. He's always been too far, and too faint."

"What do you mean, he's tried making contact?"

"He's been in my dreams. Asking for my help."

"Why your help? Cause he's handicapped?"

"He's not handicapped! I'm pretty sure they keep him drugged. He seems really, really powerful. He was able to read you, through the drugs, and through my shield. Not just anyone can do that."

That suddenly worries me.

"What do you mean, read me? What did he read?"

"Your intent to escape. He says you can do it. He says if we help him, he can help us."

"Weren't you supposed to stop that from happening?"

"I just told you. He's way too powerful, much more powerful than me, even with the drugs."

I sigh. That's not too reassuring. But I guess it's the best he can do, and if that guy can help us, then so be it.

"Ok, ok. So how are we supposed to help him, and how can he help us?"

He makes an uncertain face, biting his lip, and looks at the door again.

"We have to get him off his IV."

"Oh, just that. And how are we supposed to do that, exactly?"

"Well, maybe... I might have some kind of an idea."

"What is it?"

He looks sad, and presses the heels of his hands against his eyes.

"It's really, really risky... I'm not sure..."

"Well, what needs to be done? Can I help? And more importantly, is it worth it?"

"A psychic of that caliber? It's definitely worth it. As to how... well, maybe if you came with me..."

I shrug, trying to be encouraging. I don't want to show how annoyed I am at all this beating around the bush, even though he can probably tell.

"Well, two people are definitely better than just one."

"All right. We should try to sneak out. Tonight. And sneak into his room."

I raise an eyebrow. That's it? What was the big deal?

"Um, that's it?"

"Well, it's more complicated than that! There's cameras in the hall, and guards that make rounds."

I sigh inwardly.

"Fine, so is there a way to avoid the cameras?"

"I guess I know where they all are, so we can avoid them, and he knows the code to the lock on his door, so he can tell me and we can open it. There's just the guards to worry about."

"All right, well I suppose they make rounds?"

"Yeah."

"So we could just wait for them to go by once, and then we'd know they weren't due for a while, right?"

He nods, looking like he's considering it. He sighs, and looks up at me nervously.

"Come with me?"

I frown a bit.

"Me? What can I do?"

"You can prevent me from peeing myself?"

I chuckle. This guy can be pretty funny when he wants to be. And I've never been really good at trusting someone else with my fate, especially someone I hardly know. If something important needs to be done, I'd rather do it myself.

"Fine. Besides, I wanna meet this guy. He better be as good as you say he is."

PROBABLY DAY 10, 11:36 PM

Clay just opens the door and, after taking a look down the hallway, walks out. I guess the guards are gone; he insisted on listening to them with his mind, so I'm going to have to trust him on that. I can't believe they don't lock the doors. But then again, with super people who can just teleport or walk through walls, I don't suppose there's much of a point to an old-fashioned lock on a doorknob. I look at him, and he signals me frantically, so I hurry, imitating his movements. I look around, and I can't see a camera. But if he says they're there, and he knows how to avoid them, I'm gonna follow him close. I'm just hoping the guards don't make their rounds too close together.

We follow the walls on different sides of the hall all the way down to the electronically locked door the wheelchair guy disappeared into at the end of the hall. There, Clay slides over to lean his back against the door, and closes his eyes, looking like he's concentrating. I look around. I'm pretty nervous; now that I'm actually doing this, it seems like an even worse idea than it did originally. This guy better be worth the risk I'm taking right now. If I get caught, I'll be shipped right back to the cell they first stuck me in, and then I'll really be powerless and stuck, and I imagine it'll take a lot more time to get them to trust me again. Clay is still leaning on the door, doing nothing. It feels like it's already been a really long time.

"Clay! What are you doing?"

"Shh!"

I sigh, and look down the hall again. That's it. We're stuck, we came for nothing. Then, suddenly, Clay turns around and punches a bunch of numbers on the keypad, like he knows what he's doing, and, sure enough, the light on the lock turns green and the door clicks open. I follow Clay inside, and I'm about to shut the door behind us when I realize that there's no keypad inside, so I leave it open, just a crack, to make sure we don't get trapped, hoping to whatever god Mister Lupino believes in that this isn't going to take long enough for us to get caught by guards.

The room's even emptier than the cell they first gave me. It doesn't even have a metal toilet in the wall, just a bed and nothing else except the wheelchair I first saw the guy we came for in. He's awake, staring at Clay, who's fiddling with his IV, just below the machine that I guess counts how much of which bag is going in the tube.

"You know what you're doing?"

Clay looks at me, and then at the guy, and shrugs.

"He seems to. Looks like it might work. It's better than what I would have come up with; I have to block what's going to his veins while making sure the liquid still goes somewhere."

He finishes whatever it is he's doing with the IV tube, and then goes to sit on the floor.

"What are you doing? If you did what you came here for, then we gotta get out of here!"

"Well... don't you wanna talk to him?"

"Isn't he a super-psychic or something? Couldn't he talk to us even though we're not here?"

Clay blinks and shakes his head.

"Yeah. Of course. I must be tired."

He stands up again, and I follow him out of the room. We shut the door, and start to walk close to the walls again, and I bump into Clay as he comes to a dead stop. I'm about to tell him to watch it, when I see what made him stop. There's a couple of guards in weird-looking black uniforms, with stun guns on their hips, walking down the hall towards us. They don't seem to have noticed us yet, but it's only a matter of seconds; I mean, there's nowhere to go. I start concentrating, preparing for a hard fight. I know I'm caught, and I'm done for, and I'm going back to that damn cell, but I sure as hell ain't going there without a fight. There's a chance I won't win, though; these guards are supers, and who knows what else we'll encounter before we find our way out of this place? Or get lost unprepared and disoriented, in the woods I saw outside? Either way, it looks pretty grim.

But the guards keep on walking. And not noticing. And walking further. And still not noticing us. And they're walking, and walking... and walking... and walk right past us. I don't make a sound, but I do notice Clay is concentrating so hard he's sweating, staring at the guards. They walk out of the building, past the high-security doors that'll take them to the hallway that overlooks the woods, and Clay almost collapses on me. I help him stay upright.

"You ok, man?"

"I'll be fine. That took a lot out of me. Let's get back, I need to lie down."

I support him as we make our way back to our room, and help him get in and lie down on his bed. He looks kind of pale, but he's less clammy than he was in the hall.

"So... what happened out there... some kind of mind trick you pulled on them?"

He smiles at me, laying his arm across his forehead.

"Something like that. I actually call it my Jedi mind trick. I made them think we weren't there. It's not that hard, really. You go for the reality they expect. They didn't expect to find anyone in the hall. So I convinced them that they didn't."

"Pretty handy."

"I think so."

I can see in his eyes that he's starting to drift off, so I let him sleep, and I go to bed too. Today was a long day. But a good day.

SOMETIME DURING THE NIGHT BETWEEN DAY 10 AND DAY 11

Nicolas is in his swing, his face contorted in concentration as he reaches above his head with his little arms, batting at the plastic animals in his mobile. He manages to catch one, and he lights up in a huge smile, giggling in his high little voice that sounds like bells. He's always so happy to catch things. I smile at him and drink my coffee, watching Mister Lupino lean down over the swing and speak Italian to him. Mister Lupino has been insisting Nicolas should learn Italian if I won't. I don't think that's very fair. I've been doing my best to learn. I'm just not that smart.

The swing looks odd in Lupino's living room, like it doesn't belong there, and I wonder at that for a moment. Then I shrug it off. What does it really matter what belongs where? I frown. The guy sitting in the other couch across from me definitely doesn't belong here. I don't even know him. Or do I? He's familiar. Is he one of the kids Luke is taking care of? He looks around. I don't like him doing that; this is my place.

"So. This is your happy place, is it? Weird. I expected something more extreme. Or exotic. Goes to show, you really never can be sure."

"Who are you?"

"I'm Tom. You came to help with my IV. I thought we should talk. But you were sleeping, and I didn't want to bother you, so... I thought I'd meet you here."

I stand when I realize that this is just in my head, that Lupino and Nicolas aren't really here, and they disappear. Then I realize that I'm not really standing, that I'm not really anywhere, in fact, and everything else disappears, leaving us standing in darkness. Tom is still sitting, on nothing, like none of this happened, and he looks around, eyebrows raised.

"Boy. You're a pretty pragmatic guy, aren't you."

"I don't like being lied to."

He raises an eyebrow, leaning his head in his hand and his elbow on an invisible table.

"Who's lying? All this is in your head, and that's where we are. But if you want to do it this way, it's up to you."

I fold my arms and wait for him to talk. I might have helped free the guy, and I understand why he's talking to me, but showing me images of the people I miss most was kind of an unnecessary cheap shot, and I'm not in an open minded mood anymore.

"You know, it wasn't me that chose to show you all these things. I just picked whatever seemed to be the happiest place in your mind, and that was it. I wanted to make you feel relaxed and comfortable, because I feel everything that you feel, and I enjoy being relaxed and comfortable."

Of course, he's hearing everything that I'm thinking. He's in my head. We're both in my head. I guess he has a point. I want to sit down and listen, and suddenly I am sitting, back on one of Lupino's leather couches. He smiles.

"Good. So let's go back to where we started, shall we? Thank you for helping Clay come to my aid. I would have never been able to convince him without you. When I saw you in the hall... I saw that my time had finally come."

"What do you mean?"

"I needed someone with your strength of mind. And your particular capacities."

"What, you mean making fire?"

"No. I mean being able to take action without your power. Being a leader. And caring for others. It's a rare combination that you have."

"Ok... so what'll you need me to do?"

"I need your help for two things. First of all, when the time comes and we are ready to go, I will need some assistance to physically get out from my bed and out of the building."

"Why? You mean you actually, really can't move?"

"Not at the moment. Normally, yes, I can talk, move, walk... But they've been pumping me full of drugs for nearly five years now, and I'm afraid I'm not able to stand on my own."

"Ok, well, of course, you got it. Next?"

"I need you to take out the null."

"The what?"

"The man you know as Harvey. That's what his power is. He's what we call an area null. He can negate other people's powers, just by being there."

"Oh. Well. I had noticed. I just didn't know the word for it. So, what, you want me to kill him?"

I'm not sure I could do it. This guy might piss me off because of what he can do, but he's done nothing that deserves being killed over. Not that I know of, anyway. Like before, Tom answers without me having to say anything.

"Don't worry. I don't need you to kill him. Simply render him unconscious, and his power will stop working. And yours will start again. That's all I need. I can take care of the rest."

I raise an eyebrow. Is this guy really that powerful? Even in my mind, he doesn't look older than, like twelve. What can he do, all by himself?

"Actually, I'm thirteen, not that age is relevant to capabilities, which is something you should know. But what I can do is read everyone's thoughts and communicate with everyone. That's all anyone really needs to lead a revolution."

"Sounds like you've been planning this a while."

"I have. And I need a little while longer to make contact with everyone we could use. Not every super working for GenEx is going to be on our side, but a vast majority is. So all you have to do right now, is plan for how you will take care of the null. When you have it, I will know, and when the time is right for everything, I will give the signal."

"I don't understand, though. What do we do after that?"

"I will be giving instructions to everyone about their part of the operation. It should take minutes, at the most. And if I manage to do all I want to tonight, it should happen tomorrow."

"What about the other psychics? Won't they know you're talking to us? I mean, Clay said they monitored things."

He has a smile I've seen before, on the face of people like Jimmy, when they're about to do something that's simultaneously real bad, but that's gonna feel real good. It looks all sorts of wrong on a kid this young, and I suddenly wonder what I've unleashed.

"They will not know. I know how to deal with them. There's a reason they've kept me sedated all those years, you know. But don't worry. You have nothing to worry about from me."

I nod. I might as well trust him; he's my best ticket out of here, if what he says is true.

"All right. I'll wait for your signal."

PROBABLY DAY 11, 7:35 AM

Someone is shaking me awake, and I was sleeping so deeply it takes me a while to recognize Clay.

"Alex! Wake up!"

"Huh? What? What's going on?"

"Nothing, not right now, but did he talk to you in your dreams, too?"

I blink at him.

"You, too?"

"Yeah!"

I sit up, rubbing my face. Why am I so tired?

"So, what did he say to you?"

163

"He thanked me for helping him. And then he said he had a plan for getting us out of here, and that I should wait for his signal. What did he tell you?"

I yawn and stretch. How many people has this guy contacted last night? In any case, it looks like he's already getting a move on. Good. I can't wait to be out of here.

"Pretty much the same thing."

Clay grins. He seems real excited, and I can't help but smile.

"It's really gonna happen, isn't it?"

"It's sure starting to look that way."

We get dressed and head over to the cafeteria, where the mood is completely different than it has been for the past two days. Everyone's quiet, and thoughtful, and I find myself wondering if Tom's been in their dreams too. He said he'd explain his plan to everyone that was on our side. How do I know who that is? Is it all of them? Some? Any? We grab our trays, and get served a bowl of the same tasteless oatmeal we had yesterday, and while Clay goes to join his table, I go sit with the four I've been sitting with. Russell didn't speak to me all day yesterday after I beat him, giving me the cold shoulder in, I think, some obscure, ineffective attempt at regaining his leadership. I tried to make him understand I wasn't interested in taking his place, but that only seemed to make matters worse. Today, though, he just seems preoccupied. I'm glad the pissing contest is over, but I can't help but wonder if he was contacted last night, and what he thought. What he's thinking now. He seemed to think this place was all right. All the others are quiet and thoughtful, too; in fact, even Speedy doesn't seem to be as jumpy as usual.

"Hey. You guys ok?"

They look at me, and at each other. No one says anything for a while, and then Naomi leans in to whisper at me so low, I can barely hear her.

"We all had weird dreams, last night."

Bingo. If they all had the dreams, then they're all willing to help. Right? I keep my voice as low as I can, looking around to make sure no one else is listening, and work hard to keep my face neutral.

"Oh? What kind of weird dreams?"

"Well... about some guy. Talking to us. Did you have one too?"

I suddenly have the paranoid thought that she's trying to trap me into admitting something. Is she a psychic spy? Then I remember that her power is a supersonic scream, and I try to relax a little. If we're going to work as a team, some level of trust is going to have to be involved.

"Yeah. I did. And yeah, it's real."

Russell looks at me. He looks half worried, half really pissed off.

"Well! What are we supposed to do about it? I mean sure, get out, but what do we do after?"

I look around nervously. It wasn't that loud, but I don't want anyone to hear us. There's no one else in the room but us, though. Even the lunch ladies have retreated back to their kitchen. I'm about to comment, when Jill hits him on the forearm.

"Keep it down, will ya?"

Speedy leans in and nods, really quickly. I cringe, but when he speaks, he's actually a lot quieter than I thought him capable of.

"Yeah! It doesn't matter, where we go, go, as long as we go! Right? Right, Alex?"

They all turn to me. I glance at Russell, but even he is looking at me expectantly, as if I hold all the answers, and I wonder if he realizes that they've all suddenly and unexpectedly made me leader, even him. I stay quiet for too long, cause Naomi sighs, apparently deciding that maybe I don't know anything after all.

"I agree with Russell. I want out of here, but where would I go? I'd be a fugitive. If they caught me, they'd send me back to juvie. Or here. Anyway, I can't really go back home. And it's not like I'm the only one; some of us don't even have homes to go back to. This is all we have left, however pathetic this is."

Being a leader. And caring for others. It's a rare combination you have.

I blink when I hear Tom's voice in my head, and I'm not sure if it's a memory or him really talking to me, but I suddenly understand something he needs me for, something he didn't say in so many words. It's one thing to get out of here. Julie mentioned that staying out was quite another. I guess this is where I come in.

"What if I told you I had a place for you to go after we break out? Something for you to do?"

There's plenty of room at the old house, and Luke and them can help each other, as long as they understand the rules. As for jobs, I can put them to work there, or a lot of other good places. I can think of many, many things people like Russell and Naomi would be good at. Naomi frowns.

"Like what?"

"Like any number of things. It depends what you want to do. But I run a... sort of shelter for kids who have nowhere else to go. They can go to school if they want. If not, well... there's always what I do for a living."

"What? Didn't you just say you ran a shelter?"

"Yeah, but it's not my full-time job."

"What do you mean, full-time job? How old are you?"

I smile a little, despite myself. It's a source of pride for me, what I've managed to accomplish in my relatively short life.

"I'm seventeen."

"Well, don't you go to school?"

I shake my head.

"I haven't gone to school since 6th grade. What, did you think I was just stupid? I didn't learn the stuff you guys did to prepare for whatever the hell Harvey's talking about in class."

They look at each other, like they're trying to decide what to believe, and then Naomi raises an eyebrow at me.

"Don't your parents make you go?"

I keep my face neutral. They don't need to know that that's not a fun thing for me to discuss.

"I don't have any. I haven't for a while. Anyway, that's not really the point."

"What about social services, then?"

"They never found me. It's complicated."

"Well, how'd you get a job, then?"

"Well, it's all in what I do. I took over what used to be a Russian mob outfit, and now I run it under the Lupino syndicate, in New Cambridge."

I take a sip of the vile instant coffee they serve, but it's all right. I do it for the effect, not the taste. They all stare at me, and I can tell they're trying to decide if I'm telling the truth. Russell's the first to speak.

"Bullshit."

I shrug, like what they think doesn't really concern me, and really, it doesn't, except for the fact that I need them to decide to help us get out.

"Believe what you like. But the bottom line is, I have the means to offer you something real when we get out. Financially, and otherwise."

They look at each other for a long enough time that I'm wondering if they're communicating telepathically too, but Naomi only raises her eyebrows and shrugs one shoulder as if to say, 'why not?' to which Russell eventually sighs, and nods.

"All right. But if we get out and you're full of shit, I'm going to beat the crap out of you, fire or no fire. Don't forget I'm invulnerable, and I'm not going to let you pull that little trick on me again."

That reminds me of myself so much, I smile.

"Deal."

At that very moment, I look over Russell's shoulder, spotting the drill sergeant that passes for a gym instructor walking in the cafeteria, and I put down my spoon. It doesn't matter that I haven't had time to eat. Much more important things have been taken care of.

PROBABLY DAY 11, 1:41 PM

It's oddly satisfying to be sitting in class, listening to Harvey teach us math, and keeping my mind busy coming up with workable ways to knock out the teacher. Of course, I've gone around all the available options in minutes, and the best one is really the first one, but visualizing myself beating the crap out of him is a lot more fun and useful than trying to understand his algebra thing. I sat in front today, and he was suspicious at first, but I'm making a confused face and really pretending to listen, so he's moved on from being suspicious to probably thinking I've become a model pupil. I wonder if it'll happen today. I hope Tom has got all his ducks in a row pretty soon, 'cause I don't know how much longer I can keep up this interested student act.

As if on cue, I hear his voice in my head, exactly like this morning at the cafeteria, or yesterday when Clay spoke to me in my mind.

Now, Alex. Take him out.

I smile, and stretch, cracking my back. After all this time, all this humiliation, and all this frustration, this is going to feel really good. As I stand, I concentrate on all the anger I feel towards this place, at being locked up, at being separated from my son, at not knowing how Lupino's faring without me, at how they've treated me since I got here. Not that I'm going to make any fire with Harvey still conscious, but anger's always good for a beating. Harvey watches me come, and I see hesitation, then panic in his eyes as he reads my expression.

"Sit back down this instant. What do you think you're doing?"

I try to keep my posture relaxed, and I shrug, as if to say I don't know, before turning the movement into my best right hook. He doesn't see it coming, and I get him square between the eyes. He falls to the floor. I test my fire. Still nothing; he's gotta still be conscious.

Without waiting, I get down on the ground and start wailing on him. He puts up his arms to defend himself, so I punch him in the gut to have him bring them back down, before hitting him in the head again, aiming for the temple, trying to knock him out. I know what I'm doing: I've seen Jimmy kill plenty of people with just his fists, and though I don't really mean to kill this guy, I will if I have to. When my fist is good and bloody, I test my fire again. At last, flames come roaring out of my hands. I quickly press my fingers on his throat, right at the left corner of his jaw, and feel a faint pulse there. Good. I didn't kill him. I'm surprised at how relieved that makes me feel, but I have to push the thought out of my head; this is no time for doubting myself. I wipe the blood from my hand on his shirt, and I stand, turning to my classmates. They're all staring at me, wide-eyed, even

Russell. Funny; I would have thought he'd be more desensitized to violence than that.

"Well, what are you waiting for? Didn't you get the signal?"

They look at each other, and they all stand at almost exactly the same time. I'm relieved; I was worried I'd have to take on some of them. Not that I couldn't, I just didn't want to. I wait for further instruction, but then Clay takes the lead, running to the front of the class.

"Ok, come on, this way!"

He runs out, and down the hall, and though some are hesitant, I can see everyone's following him. We go past the gym doors, and we reach the door to Tom's room, where Clay punches the code on the keypad. I hear Tom's voice in my head telling me to come in, and see the others taking strategic positions to defend the room, so I guess Tom must be talking to them, too. It's really weird to think we're all hearing different orders from the same person, but none of us know what he's saying to the others. At least, I think that's the way it is. I don't have time to think too much about it, though. I walk in.

He looks a lot sicker and frailer than the boy I saw in my dream. He's whiter than the sheets on his bed, except for the black circles under his eyes, and he's so skinny I can see the shape of his bones. He smiles at us, and I hear his voice in my head again, telling me to help him up. I go to the bed while Clay gets the wheelchair from the corner and pushes it over to where we are. Tom's real light when I pick him up and put him in the chair, so much so that I almost fall backwards when I lift him. When he's sitting, he flexes his hands and grabs the arms of the wheelchair, clumsily, like he's not used to moving. He looks at me, and I hear his voice in my head telling me to take him outside. I raise an eyebrow and fold my arms.

"You said you could do all sorts of normal things. Now, I'm willing to push you 'cause I see you're in no shape, but there's no way I'm putting up with this creepy head-talk shit. Got me?"

He smiles like I've said something he likes to hear, and his voice is dry and cracked like he hasn't had a drink of water in years, which I suppose is possible.

"Fine. I promise I'll talk to you out loud when you're in range. But for now, you're going to have to put up with a bit more... head-talk, until we're out. All right?"

I nod.

"Deal. Clay, can you push him? I think I'll be more useful fighting, if we have to."

Clay grabs the handles in the back of the chair.

"Yeah. And we will. I think there are guards coming."

I step outside in front of them, and I see that he's right. There's four guys coming, including the huge fuck that threw me against the wall that time. They're taking out their guns, pointing them on my new friends. One of them fires at Jill, not bullets but weird darts, but they go right through her. Russell yells, grabs the gun, and rams the butt of it in the guy's chin. I'm about to take on immovable, superstrong Will, but then I see he's grabbing one of his fellow guards into a bear hug, squeezing him. I don't know what to make of it for a little while, and then I remember what Tom said about contacting everyone that was on our side. I guess that means there were a lot more than just us prisoners, including people who might have not had a choice. I wonder how many guards are suddenly fighting among themselves, and realize for the first time that escaping here might be a lot easier than I imagined. Russell's beating the crap out of the guy who shot at Jill, and Naomi and the Chinese guy I was never formally introduced to are combining supersonic scream and wind power to take down a guy who can apparently fly. So far, this is going well. I see that I'm not needed after all, and I turn back to Clay and Tom.

"So, what next?"

"He says to go get your friend Julie. Who's Julie?"

I blink. I did remember about her, but I didn't expect him to know. Just how strong is this guy? I see the guards left the high-security doors open, and I start running towards them. The others follow me through them, and down the hall where you can see the forest on either side. When we reach the research building, though, I can see I'm the only one that takes the direction of the cells; everyone else is splitting into two groups, heading in different directions. I hesitate, like I'm not doing what I'm supposed to, and I hear Tom's voice telling me to keep moving, so I do. It's the weirdest thing, working together for a common goal and having no clue what the others are up to.

It takes me a while to get there, because I get turned around twice, but I made the trip so often from the cell to the room where they made me practice that when I find that, I know exactly which way to go, and I find my old cell in no time. I stop in front of what must be Julie's door, and knock on it real hard.

"Julie?"

There's silence on the other side for a few seconds, and I'm starting to think that I'm in the wrong place after all, but then she finally answers me.

"Alex? Is that you?"

"Yeah, it's me! I've come to get you! We're breaking out, like, now!"

"... really? Well, I gotta give you some credit, kid!"

"I'm not a kid! Do you want to stay where you are?"

"All right, all right. Well, what are you waiting for?"

I look at the door. There are two bolts and an electronic lock on it.

"Uh... I'm not sure how I'm gonna do it."

"Ugh! You're useless. So much for the big hero rescue. Kill the EM field generator, and I can come out."

"How do I do that?"

"Do you see a black box on the wall next to the lock on my door?"

I look around. There is one, about the size of my head, with a knob on it.

"Uh, yeah?"

"Is there a switch, or something?"

"There's a knob."

"Great. Turn it down until it clicks. That should do it."

I try it. There's only one way the knob will turn, and, sure enough, when I turn it all the way, something clicks.

"Ok!"

She doesn't reply. I press my ear against the door, trying to hear what she's doing.

"Julie?"

I jump when someone taps my shoulder, but when I turn around, it's just a girl, grinning and waving at me. She's real tall, as tall as I am, which is pretty tall for a girl, and her hair is strawberry-blonde, redder than mine. She's got green eyes, and the trace of what used to be freckles on her nose; she's also a lot younger than what I expected, only in her mid-twenties or so. Definitely not old enough to be calling me kid. She's looking me up and down appreciatively, in the way that Lori did the first time she met me, and every time she's about to take my clothes off.

There's a weird, squeezing kind of feeling in my chest when I think of Lori and, again, I put it out of my mind so I can stay efficient. She grins and trails a finger down my chest.

"Hmm, turns out you're not as young as I thought you would be. Pretty good-looking, too."

I turn to look down the hall to make sure she doesn't see me blush.

"Uh, we have to get going."

"Yeah, well I got something to do."

"Like what?"

"There's a guy talking to me in my head who told me you were coming. Turns out, he also wants me to do something specific."

I raise my eyebrows. Tom really has been talking to everyone. I have to admit that I had my doubts about this whole thing, but the closer we get to escaping, the more impressed I am. She starts down the hall, and I follow her. She passes three cells, stops in front of one to look at the number, then just disappears. I look around stupidly for a little while, and then she's back, suddenly standing next to me holding a brown-haired girl who looks as confused as I feel. The girl blinks at me, and apparently dismisses me, cause she starts walking away. Julie raises her eyebrows and calls after her.

"Uh, you're welcome!"

The girl doesn't stop, just keeps marching, and I hear Tom's voice telling me to follow her. So does Julie, obviously, because she starts following her too. The girl reaches the end of the hall, and turns into a hallway that I've never been in before.

"Uh, hey, unknown girl, do you know where you're going?"

She turns to give me a funny look, like I'm a talking dog, for just a moment, before continuing.

"I am Clara. Server room. 137 meters south-south-west. It should take us approximately one minute seventeen seconds to reach our destination."

I turn to look at Julie.

"Approximately."

She shrugs, and we keep following the girl for, apparently, 137 meters, until we reach the hall where Finley's office was. Clara stops in front of a door that's bolted shut with three different kinds of locks, and turns to Julie.

"You need to get me inside."

Julie shrugs, and smiles at me.

"Don't go anywhere, handsome. I'll be right back."

I'm glad she disappears with Clara then, because I have no idea how to answer, and I find it very annoying that all the pretty girls I meet try to make me as uncomfortable as humanly possible.

As soon as they're gone, I hear Tom's voice in my head.

The door directly across the hall.

I turn, to look right at Finley's office door.

Yes, that's the one. You need to break in there, and burn all the hard copies of the files they have on us.

I get to the door and kick it down almost effortlessly. The office is pretty much as I remember. There are a few filing cabinets against the far wall that I hadn't noticed my first time here, though; I suppose I was pretty distracted. There's also a closet next to them, and I decide to take a look inside. There's not a lot there, a few boxes, a suitcase, a coat. One of the boxes is labeled A.W., so I pick it up and check it out.

My stuff's all there. Well, my clothes aren't, but they were pretty trashed. My wallet, my keys, my phone, it's all there, even the silver cigarette case that Lori gave me.

I stare at it, and it's the first time it really hits me; I'm getting out, it's happening, I'm going to get to see them again. My family. I never thought I could miss them so much. I open the case, but of course, there's no cigarettes inside. I snap it shut, and I'm so stressed out and angry that burning the contents of the file cabinets happens practically by itself.

I check my cell phone on the way out, but the battery's dead, and I didn't have my charger on me when I was taken. I pocket it anyway.

I'm alone in the hallway, so I go and knock on the bolted door to see if the girls are still in there.

"Julie?"

"Alex? Hold your horses, we're not done yet."

I lean on the door, and wait, and I swear it hasn't been more than a minute when I feel a warning from Tom, and I hear a bunch of people running down the hall. It's three people, the two guys who grabbed me off the street, and Greasy Snake in person. I smile to myself. It's payback time. I practically need no concentration at all to make a huge blast of fire in their direction. These guys deserve everything I've got to throw at them. Even better, the carpet catches fire, so when I throw another blast, it's even larger, and hotter. The little guy is standing in front of greasy snake, but the big one is making his weird hand gestures again, not at me, but at my fire, and the flames go out like he just blew out the candles on a cake. I glare at him. Fine. I guess his taking out the air trick doesn't just work on lungs. But I've got other tricks up my sleeve, too. I start to heat up his body. I can do that until he bursts in ash, but he counterattacks right away, pulling the air from my lungs, and it becomes a struggle to see if I can burn him alive before he can make me pass out from lack of oxygen. Unfortunately, as my vision starts to turn blurry, I lose my grip on my anger, and so, on my fire, and I see I'm gonna lose this stupid fight.

As I'm about to pass out, I see Julie reappear and grab the big one by the neck, and suddenly, there's air for me to breathe again. I gasp and wheeze for breath, and as Julie disappears with the big guy I see the small one running towards me, reaching out a hand to touch me. I manage to roll to the side before he can take my power away, and thinking that this is the bastard that took me away from my son, it's child's play to throw a blast of fire intense enough that I'm not sure if he's alive or dead when he collapses on the floor. I don't check 'cause I don't really want to know, and I turn to the other dude, Finley, the greasy snake. Julie's already there, holding him by the necktie and beating the crap out of him. I watch her go for a few seconds, surprised; she packs a hell of a punch, for a girl. Eventually, Finley stops whimpering, and Julie lets him fall to the floor. Her fist is as bloody as mine was after I got done with Harvey, but she doesn't seem bothered by it. I stand up, nodding at her.

"Thanks. Where's the other dude?"

She grins at me.

"He won't be bothering us again. I put him somewhere safe."

"Good. Useful power."

"Yeah, no kidding."

I motion to Finley with my chin.

"He dead?"

She shakes her head.

"Nah. Tom wants me to bring him alive."

I jump when I hear a pounding coming from the locked door next to me, and I curse myself for being such a scaredy cat when I hear Clara's voice on the other side.

"I'm done! Get me out!"

Julie rolls her eyes, disappears, and reappears holding Clara. I look at the room.

"What were you doing in there, anyways?"

She sighs audibly, rolling her eyes, like I'm an idiot.

"Obviously, I was irreversibly wiping their databases and erasing all traces of our identities over the entire network."

"Oh. Right. Well. That makes sense."

Julie walks over to greasy snake, and pokes him with her foot. He groans, and she looks at me.

"Can you carry him?"

I shrug and pick him up, throwing him across my shoulders in a fireman hold. He's not as heavy as I would have expected.

"Sure, no problem. Where to now?"

"The hangar. Clara, can you take us there?"

She nods.

"304 meters north-north-east, compensating for stairs and hallway turns."

"Alright, well, lead the way."

She starts walking, and Julie and I follow her, towards where the scientists and officials had their offices. It's a lot more comfortable and decorated than any part of either building I've seen so far. We cross that entire area, a lot further than I've ever been, and though we do come across the occasional dead or passed out guard, there doesn't seem to be anyone around to try and stop us. We finally reach an area that looks a bit more industrial, with open doors that seem to lead to small warehouses, and Clara takes us all the way down the hall to a set of double doors that lead to a large garage. Everyone's there, and quite a few more people I've never met before. They seem to be splitting up in teams, boarding large, military transport jeeps, and leaving. When we reach the group, the only ones left are Clay, Jill, Russell, Naomi, the Asian guy, and Tom, waiting next to the last vehicle. Tom looks at me, and I dump greasy snake at his feet. The man moans, and tries to get up, but when he sees Tom looking at him, he scrambles backwards, bumping into my legs.

"Tom...! How did you... we can talk about this. There are so many things..."

Tom's eyes swivel to me in that terrifying way that they have, and I hear him in my mind, a lot louder and clearer than usual, ordering me to bring him Finley so hard I feel almost compelled to do it. I grab him by the upper arm and drag him to Tom, who lifts one of his skeletal hands to lay it on the guy's forehead. Greasy snake begs, and then just screams, a blood-curdling scream of terror and pain that I wouldn't even wish on this guy. Tom must have a serious issue with him to do whatever it is he's doing.

I let him go when he seems to be done, and greasy snake falls seated on his ass, staring at us with expressionless, wide eyes. He opens his mouth, and I'm sure he's gonna say something, but the only thing that comes out is a long string of drool. I want to know what's wrong with him, but right now, I don't dare ask, and I can see I'm not the only one uncomfortable with what just happened. Julie is the first one to snap out of it, and I can guess that it's really Tom asking her to do something, because she looks at him before speaking.

"Right! Let's get out of here. Everyone in the truck. I'm driving."

We all climb in the back, and I help Russell get the wheelchair in before taking a seat myself. Clay and Jill look out excitedly through the plastic windows in the canvas that covers the back, and even Russell and Naomi seem pretty happy. But when I think of all the problems my absence has probably caused, I only feel tired. When I close my eyes to get some rest, I see Nicolas, and I'm glad he's not old enough to ask any questions yet.

OCTOBER 21ST, 4:53 PM

"Hello?"

I sigh in relief. Jimmy and Lori didn't pick up when I called; I'm glad at least Luke isn't crazy about having to recognize the number on the caller I.D.

"Luke?"

"Holy crap, Alex, is that you?"

I have to smile. It's so good to be hearing his voice.

"Yeah, it's me."

"Where have you been? We thought you were dead!"

Julie glances at me from the driver's seat, but I don't look at her. This is my business.

"Well, I'm not. I've just... well, it's a really, really long and complicated story. I'm on my way, now, and I have a lot of people with me that are going to need some stuff."

"Stuff? People? What are you talking about? Where are you, what's going on?"

"Calm down. I'm with some friends. They were trapped in the same place I was, and now we all need some clothes. Can you do that?"

"What kind of clothes? What size?"

I have to hand it to Luke; he's pretty good at giving me what I need and asking questions later.

"Just grab some of the emergency money and go get a bunch of sweatpants and t-shirts, some large, some small, some medium, and that should hold everyone off until I can fix something more permanent."

"Fine. Fine. I'll send someone. When will you be here?"

"I don't know. An hour or so."

"Ok, we'll hurry."

"Thanks."

"Sure. I'm just glad you're alive."

I smile as I hang up the phone, then try the condo again. There's no answer. I feel that familiar anxiety rising up and squeezing my chest, but I shake it off. She never answers the phone when she doesn't recognize the caller I.D.; she doesn't like picking up when it's one of my guys or mister Lupino on a burner phone. You'd think she'd be more anxious about the phone since I've been missing so long, though. A thought occurs to me. What if my guys gave her trouble? Would they? I'm sure Luke would have told me if he knew something was wrong. Wouldn't he?

Julie pulls me out of my thoughts.

"So, what did your friend say?"

"He's expecting you. He's sent someone to go get us clothes."

"Efficient."

"Yeah. That's Luke, all right."

I hand her back the phone she loaned me, and she looks at it like it's covered in shit.

"That's not mine. It was just here."

I shrug, and drop it on the seat between us. Julie steals glances at me as she drives, and raises an eyebrow.

"You ok?"

I sigh, and nod.

"I'll be fine. I'm just tired."

"I expected you'd be more excited than this."

"Me too. I just never had the time to think about how much shit I'd have to take care of while I was in there. Now I realize."

"You should try to relax, you know, live day by day."

"Believe me, I do. It's just, today's the day that I have to clean the shit that hit the fan while I was gone."

She smiles and shakes her head slightly.

"I can help out. I'm pretty good at fixing problems, you know."

"It's fine. I don't even know how much I'll have to do yet. Besides, if you really do want to help out, you can help Luke take care of everyone."

"Why? What will you be doing?"

"I gotta go home. I need to take care of some personal stuff, and I gotta take care of my business."

"Oh, so you're not coming with us? Won't your friend be pissed that he has to deal with a bunch of strangers?"

I glare at her. How's this her business, anyway?

"Luke understands what I have to do."

"Fine, fine, whatever you say."

We stay quiet for another hour, until I have to give her directions to my place.

"So, I can't change your mind? You still want me to drop you off?"

"Yeah."

"All right."

She stops in front of the building, and leans over the wheel to see through the window, letting out one low whistle.

"Pretty nice. You must have a lot of money."

"Yeah. I do."

I open the door, and slide out of the truck, leaving it open so I can give her directions to the house.

"You gonna be ok to get there?"

"Yeah, I should be. If not, all I gotta do is hit redial, right?"

I nod and shut the door. She drives away as I walk towards the building. My neighbor is sitting on the stairs again, smoking a cigarette. I notice he's staring at me with his mouth hanging open, and I realize that I'm wearing blue scrubs that are stained with blood, and no shoes. I stop in front of him.

"Rough day. Again. Got a smoke?"

He nods with the same expression and hands me a cigarette and his lighter. I use the lighter, and give it back to him, then walk into the building with my smoke, and to hell with the no smoking sign. He doesn't say anything.

Normally, I would wonder what he's thinking, but right now, I can't bring myself to care. During the elevator ride to my floor, it occurs to me that I don't have my keys anymore, but Lori's probably there, so it doesn't matter. I try the knob when I reach the door, and predictably, it's unlocked.

I know right away that something's wrong. The place is dead quiet, and there are half packed boxes of stuff all over the place. Is she leaving?

"Lori? You there? I'm back!"

I start looking through the rooms, calling out for Lori, but there's no one there. I grab the phone and call Luke.

"Yeah?"

"Where's Lori and my kid?"

"What are you talking about? Aren't you coming here?"

"I went home to see my family. They're not there. There's boxes. The door was unlocked. What's going on? Where's Nicolas? Where's Lori?"

"We can talk about it when you're here. You told me you were coming. Are you coming?"

"Tell me. Now."

"Relax, ok? Nicolas is here. Get over here and we'll talk."

"Fine."

192

I hang up and call Jimmy. I don't like what's going on, and I can tell that Luke is refusing to give me answers until he sees me. Jimmy picks up on the first ring; I guess he saw my number on the caller I.D.

"Boss? Is that you?"

"Yeah, it's me."

"Where the fuck have you been? Do you have any idea what's been going on? You've been missing for like, two weeks! Have you called Luke?"

"Yeah, I've called Luke. It's a long story. I'm at my place. Come over."

"I'm on my way."

I hang up, strip out of the blue scrubs, and head for the shower. I think this could have been the most satisfying shower I've ever had in my life if I wasn't so stressed out about what's going on. When I come out with a towel wrapped around my waist, Jimmy's in the entrance hall, waiting for me. He looks me up and down.

"All right, so, you're not mortally hurt or missing arms and legs, so where the fuck have you been?"

I sigh and walk to the bedroom with him following me. He knows me enough to leave me my privacy while I get dressed, though, and he waits for me outside the door.

"It's complicated."

"You really think you're gonna get away with telling me vague shit like that?"

I start putting on the first suit I find.

"Fine. I was kidnapped. Don't you dare laugh."

He stays quiet, and I'm kind of glad I can't see his face right now. I don't know why he's not making fun of me, and it's making me uncomfortable, so I just go on.

"It was a sort of research lab thing where they did experiments on people with superpowers."

"What, so there are others like you?"

"Well, yeah. Of course."

I say that, but at the same time, I hadn't really thought there was anybody other than me, either. I feel kind of sorry to have lost my uniqueness.

"Anyway, I escaped. They're not coming after me."

I finish dressing, and when I come out of the room, he offers me a cigarette. I take it, lighting it with my power, and then look at him. He seems to believe me.

"You ok, though, boss?"

I nod. I think I'm ok. Nicolas and Lori are with Luke. Well, he didn't say Lori, but she's probably there too. I still want to know why there are boxes all over the place, but I doubt Jimmy knows or cares.

"I'm fine. Now tell me about my business."

"It's actually pretty good. I told everyone you had gone on vacation with your girl."

I smile a bit. With the business with Chris taken care of, I guess he could have gotten away with saying that.

"Thanks, man. I knew I could trust you. And Lupino?"

He shrugs.

"He's ok. Still around. Hasn't keeled over yet."

I punch him in the arm, and he has a smile. He looks at me sideways.

"Still, I'm surprised you haven't called him yet."

"Hey, I just got back a couple minutes ago. Give me time."

He has a bit of a smile, but again, he should be smiling more. Hell, he should be making fun of me for being kidnapped. He's not his usual self, though; something is up, and I don't understand why he doesn't just tell me. He's never beaten around the bush before.

"What is it? Did something else happen? Did someone else turn on us? Did we lose turf?"

It's another thing that could go wrong; I've always got rival gangs trying to muscle in on my territory. There's so many things to worry about that sometimes I don't even know where to start. He shakes his head, and I'm

195

only partially reassured, because the expression on his face is grim.

"No, man. I kept it up. Almost nobody really knew you were gone."

I nod. It's good I have him represent me for most things; few people expect to see me in person on any kind of regular basis.

"Then what is it?"

He looks me in the eye.

"You told me you called Luke. Didn't he tell you?"

"Tell me what?"

"You better sit down, man."

My heart is beating faster. This must be bad. Jimmy told me Lupino was fine. I know Nicolas is fine, too, because Luke said so. He also said he was with him. But he didn't say anything about Lori. I just assumed. I must have been wrong. Something's wrong with Lori. Maybe she is leaving me after all. I find the first seat available, on the couch, and sit.

"Is it Lori? Did she relapse?"

He's not looking me in the eye. This has to be bad.

"Yeah. She relapsed."

"Well, what? Is she in rehab? Did she do something to Nicolas?"

"No, man. He's fine."

He stays quiet. I can't believe he's making me linger like that.

"Well, what?"

He shakes his head, and I can tell it's really pissing him off, having to be the one to tell me this.

"She O.D.'ed, man. She's dead."

OCTOBER 21ˢᵀ, 7:17 PM

Jimmy drops me off at the house, but stays in the car like he usually does. I check myself in the mirror to make sure I don't look like I cried. I didn't cry on the way here, of course, I could never cry in front of Jimmy, but when I stepped out of the bathroom my eyes were pretty red, even if I only did it for a few minutes. I resent myself, because I swore I'd never cry again, and I hadn't for five years, but I couldn't help it. Just like I couldn't help her. I should have been there. I should have tried harder. I should have...

I shake my head, 'cause my eyes are starting to sting again, and I try to dismiss the thoughts from my mind. I know Nicolas is fine, at least. Though he might not have been. What if I hadn't happened to drop him off with Luke that day?

I'm about to walk in when the door opens and Julie, Jill and Clay step out. They're wearing the new clothes I asked Luke to buy for them, assorted one-size t-shirts and sweatpants. Julie smiles at me, looking at me in that appreciative way, and I look away. I don't feel like being hit on right now.

"Hey, good-looking. Nice suit! We're just headin' out."

"Oh? Where are you going?"

Clay smiles at me.

"I called my parents. Jill, too. They want us back. Julie's gonna drive us."

"Oh?"

He nods, and I see even shy Jill seems happy.

"We're going home."

For some reason, these words bring back the hurt, and make my throat feel tight. I have to clear it, and I walk past them, not looking at them.

"Well, keep me posted."

Julie frowns and tries to block my way.

"Hey, you ok?"

"Fine."

She squints at me.

"What is it with you and saying you're fine all the time? No, you're not. What's up?"

"Don't you have things to do?"

"Well, yeah, but…"

I push past her and walk inside. It feels good to get mad. It's familiar. She doesn't try to come after me, and I don't run into anyone in the hall.

"Luke?"

I hear running, and Luke is suddenly in front of me. He stares at me for a few seconds, during which time I have no clue what to do or say, and then he hugs me, real tight.

"Shit, Alex. It really is you. I thought you weren't coming back. I thought you were dead."

I let him hug me. I don't want to kill his moment, but I hate being hugged, and right now it's making me feel even more messed up and emotional, so it's worse than usual. He finally lets go of me, and I try for a smile. Anything to try and feel normal again. The world is still turning. Why do I feel everything in it is different, meaningless, when really, only one thing is gone? I have no idea how good my smile is, but I don't feel very convincing.

"You should give me more credit than that, man."

He looks at my face, like he's reading it, in silence. Finally, he sees what he's looking for, and he sighs and shakes his head.

"Jimmy told you."

I try to answer, but I can't find my voice, so I just nod.

"Alex, I'm so sorry."

That suddenly makes my throat hurt again, which makes me angry, and I almost yell at him, but I rein in my outburst at the last moment, managing to just sound irritated. I think.

"Don't be. It's my fault, not yours."

"Nicolas has been here all this time. Do you..."

I nod, and he takes me up the stairs. I follow him, and realize he's taking me to my old room, the only room on the third floor, next to his office, where he spends all his time. He turns the knob all the way and opens the door carefully, slowly, not making a sound. I poke my head in, ready to walk in, and I see that my boy is on his back, lying in a green foldable play-yard that looks brand new. I stare at him, and for some reason, my chest feels tight, my throat feels like I've swallowed a baseball, and my eyes burn. Why is this making me even more emotional than when Jimmy told me about Lori? What's wrong with me?

Luke watches me, and then whispers.

"I could go wake him, if you want."

I shake my head, probably a little more vigorously than I intended.

"No. No, I don't want to see him. Not right now, anyway."

Luke frowns, concern obvious on his face. For some reason, that makes me feel mad, which helps me feel calmer; angry's been my natural state for a lot of my life. He reaches to touch me, and then changes his mind, wisely.

"Are you sure? I mean..."

"Let it go, Luke."

I don't look at him as I walk out. He sighs and closes the door with as much care as he took when opening it. I walk to the stairs, taking out one of the cigarettes I bought on the way here, and light it while making my way down. How could he understand? I just can't see my son now. What the hell kind of father am I? I'm already responsible for our family being torn up, for his world falling apart, and he's not even old enough to know it yet.

Luke follows me down the stairs, but then runs to stand in front of me.

"Alex, stop for a second. Where are you going? What about Nicolas?"

It creeps up on me again, and I have to clear my throat before I speak. Stupid emotion.

"I'm not going anywhere. Couldn't smoke with him up there. So how are the new people I sent you? Do you think you can use them?"

He sighs heavily, and shakes his head, but he answers my question anyway. I sit at the bottom of the stairs, watching him. I feel so tired.

203

"The younger ones, Jill and Clay, I think, are going back home to their parents. Julie, I don't know, she's hard to gauge. Naomi and Russell manifested a desire to stay here, and I have no problem with that. It might be good for our little... community to have some diversity. Not to mention protection. You didn't tell me they were all superheroes."

I smile a little, despite the way I feel. Trust Luke to have learned everyone's name, and what there is to know about them, in so short a time. But there's someone he didn't mention.

"What about Tom?"

"Well..."

I see Luke being uncomfortable for the first time since I took this place back from the Russians. What the hell did Tom do to provoke this?

"He's a little... creepy. I wouldn't turn him down, but he says he doesn't want to stay here, and honestly it's as well this way, I think he'd freak out everyone else."

"Oh. Well. I'll find him a place somewhere, I'm sure."

Luke looks at me a bit sadly.

"What?"

"Nothing. Just... you know, Alex, not everyone you rescue is your responsibility."

"Of course they are. I can take care of them. No one else can, or will. Someone's gotta do it."

"Does it have to be you?"

I shrug and walk to the front door so I can go sit outside in peace, hoping he'll drop the subject.

"What's the point of rescuing anyone if I'm just going to abandon them afterwards? Besides, better me than nobody."

OCTOBER 21ST, 9:23 PM

I pick up the phone again, and put it back down. I've been doing that for the past hour and a half. Luke was pushy, at first, but now he's pretty much leaving me alone. I can't bring myself to do it yet. Almost being emotional in front of Jimmy was bad enough; I couldn't handle doing it with mister Lupino, even if it's over the phone. And he keeps tabs on me. He's gotta know about... about what happened when I was gone. I hear Nicolas fussing and it's like the muscles in my neck become so tense it might snap my spine; I get up and walk away. I can see Luke from the corner of my eye, sitting in a rocking chair he didn't have before, giving Nicolas his bottle, and I walk faster. I walk out the front door and sit on the steps in front of the house, taking out a cigarette and lighting it. I don't really smoke it, though; it feels like too much energy to bring it to my lips and inhale the smoke. I just put my head in my hands and feel it burn between my fingers. I stay like that for a really long time, until the cigarette has burned down to a stick of ash that's fallen on my jacket. I jump and drop the butt when Luke sits down next to me, and I realize it must have been even longer than I thought. He presses his lips into a line that's supposed to be a smile, but I can tell he doesn't have the heart for it any more than I do. I don't really want to talk, and even if I did I wouldn't know what to say, so I just grab another cigarette and light it. I actually smoke this one, and wait for him to say whatever it is he came here to say.

"I'm sure you'll feel better tomorrow. It's all just a big shock, that's all."

I frown at him. He should know better. Is he actually trying to reassure me, or himself?

"No I won't, Luke. You know that. This isn't something that time can fix."

"Of course it is. Time makes everything feel better, or at least not so bad anymore. What are you going to do, move in here and let me take care of him for the rest of his life?"

His eyes go a bit wide as he says it and he looks at me.

"You're not gonna do that, are you?"

I take another drag from my cigarette and look at the street.

"No."

He breathes a sigh of relief and has a nervous laugh.

"Oh! Good. It's just that I... well... it's not that I don't like him, just..."

"I know. He's a baby. He's trouble."

"I'm sure you'll do fine."

I shake my head.

"I won't. But that's ok. It's not gonna be me."

Luke frowns, his face contorted into something that looks halfway between worry and confusion.

"What are you talking about?"

I don't look at him, just stare at my hands.

"I can't take care of him, Luke."

There's that baseball in my throat again. I didn't really think of it, just said it, but as I say it, I know it's true. I can't do it. I can never hope to be anything better than inadequate as a father. I failed him, and I'm dangerous to be around.

"Sure you can. I know you've been weird, but it's just because you're you. I know you love him."

"That's kind of the point, actually."

"What? What do you mean?"

"I..."

I clear my throat. Stupid emotion. I can't bring myself to say it.

"I care about him. So I can't take care of him."

209

"That doesn't make any sense."

This time, I'm almost shouting. Why can't he understand this?

"Of course it does! Are you kidding? Do you know how fucked up and crazy my life is? The hours I have to put in? Or the fact that I never know if I'm gonna come home again? And now, I have crazies that are running after me just because of what I can do, I mean, I'm at the point where I have to classify all the people who want me dead into categories! I can't put him through that! That's not the kind of life he deserves!"

Luke shrugs.

"You could find a different job..."

"With no real papers? No education? No experience in anything other than terrorizing people into doing what I want them to? I'm stuck, Luke. But he doesn't have to be. Being with..."

I choke again, and I cough to cover it up. I take a drag from my smoke so long I almost cough again, but it does make me feel better.

"Trying to have a family. It worked. Or it looked like it could have. But I can't possibly be the only thing this kid has. It's not fair to him."

Luke shakes his head, but doesn't answer. I know he gets it. The only person I know who had a single dad who was a mobster is Jimmy. And for all that I care about Jimmy, there is no way I'm letting my kid turn into that. We sit quietly for another cigarette, and then Luke stands to go back inside. Before he does, though, he half turns his head to talk to me without really looking at me.

"Do me a favor, though. Before you do anything... talk to your mister Lupino about it, all right?"

I nod. Of course I'm going to talk to him about it. Just as soon as I stop being such a pussy and actually pick up the phone to call him.

OCTOBER 22ND, 9:13 AM

I take a good look at Nicolas' face while I wait for Rosanna to open the door. He's happy, grabbing at my eyebrows, my cheeks, my lips, giggling every time he manages to make me do a funny face. He's so beautiful. I can't get over how perfect he is. And soon, I won't get to look at him like that again. I take a deep breath. I can't afford to be thinking about this too much right now. The door opens, and Rosanna grins at me, her face plump and red and delirious with joy.

"Alex! And little baby! Come in, come in!"

She holds her hands out to pick up the baby, and I give him to her, though for the first time I have a hard time letting go. It's not that I don't trust her; I just feel like having him for as long as I can. She brings him into the small living room, where Lupino is sitting, reading a book. He looks good today. Of course, there's the fact that I haven't seen him in weeks, but I still think he looks better than he has for a little while. We didn't really discuss what happened while I was gone. I just called and he said to come over, so I did. I wish I had been there, for him, for Jimmy, for Luke. For Lori. I feel like I let everyone down. Especially my son.

He stands, and comes to greet me, kissing both my cheeks, wrapping his arms around me and slapping my back gently. It takes me a little by surprise; he's always been a little touchy, with touching my shoulders or arms or whatever, but he's never been quite this affectionate.

"Alex! I am so very glad to see you again, my boy. We had thought something unfortunate had happened to you. Come, have a seat."

I can hear Rosanna cooing at the baby in Italian just in the other room, so I go sit with Lupino. He's all smiles, and it makes his eyes and cheekbones wrinkle in a way I haven't seen on him since the incident last year. It's making me feel a little better, though not enough to forget about the discussion we're about to have.

"Please, tell me, how are you doing, my boy?"

He's still smiling, but his brows have gone up in the middle of his forehead, almost touching themselves, in a look of concern. I hate it when people look concerned about me. Like I have trouble handling things. I shrug.

"I'm fine. Thank you. How about you?"

He shakes his head.

"Always the stoic one, are you not, my boy? I understand how it is with our men, we cannot let them see anything other than anger. But that does not mean you cannot feel it. I wished to say... I am very sorry about your loss."

I don't look at him. I didn't tell him how Lori died. He didn't ask. I wonder if he knows. He probably does. He knows everything; he's even worse than Luke. I just stare at the table. I know he wants me to share how I feel or whatever, but even if I wanted to do that, I wouldn't really know how. I'm only capable of saying one word.

"Thanks."

He looks at the picture of his family, hanging over the fireplace.

"You know, when my wife died, I blamed myself for many, many years. For not being there at the right time. Not being there to help her."

I try to refrain from sighing. I don't want to hear how I could have done nothing, how it was beyond my control. I know that. The point is I shouldn't have been away. I shouldn't have left her.

"It is not an easy burden to live with. Even when one knows it makes no sense, it does come back to wake you in the night. And it will for many years. Just know, that if you wish to discuss it, you have someone who understands."

I look at his kind smile, not for too long, though, 'cause it makes my throat tight, and my eyes sting, and I need to get that under control. I can't lose it in front of him, I'd never forgive myself. I should have known it wouldn't be a platitude, like I hear everyone else say. There's a reason Lupino and I are so close. He gets me. I guess we really are alike, him and me.

"Thank you, Mister Lupino."

He nods once, and turns his attention to Rosanna, who's bringing him Nicolas. He takes my son, but she remains hunched over him, still talking baby talk at him in Italian before walking away, slowly, making funny faces and waving at Nicolas all the way out. Lupino watches her go, then turns his attention to my son. He talks to him softly, in Italian, for a few minutes, and then smiles at me.

"He seems well. I worried about him when I heard about your disappearance, but it seems your friend Luke has taken very good care of him."

I nod quietly, wishing I could light a cigarette. At least, with having had to go without for nearly two weeks, the cravings are easier to resist. He catches my mood, though. He settles Nicolas in his lap so that he doesn't have to be so watchful, and turns to me.

"Something is troubling you. What is it?"

I sigh and run my hand over my head.

"I... there's something I need to tell you. About Nicolas."

He frowns, but says nothing, waiting for me to go on. I bring my fingers up to my mouth to chew on the nails, but stop myself at the last minute, putting my hands down to pretend to smooth the crease on my pant leg. I have to take a deep breath before I go on.

"I've decided to give Nicolas up for adoption."

I don't dare look at him. What if he doesn't understand? What if he thinks I'm a coward? Abandoning my son? What if it changes the way he sees me? There's silence, for a long time. All I can hear is Nicolas, gurgling and sighing and breathing, and it feels a little bit ironic. I'm glad he doesn't understand, and I'm not, at the same time. Will he blame me when he grows up? Will he think I made the right choice? I look at Nicolas, and notice that mister Lupino is watching me. He doesn't look angry, or disappointed, or shocked. He just looks serious, and a little sad. His face softens when he sees me looking at him, and he sighs.

"Alex, my boy... I know you have suffered a great loss. But you should not make any rash decisions."

I shake my head.

"I'm not, mister Lupino. I've thought about it really carefully, as carefully as I ever thought about anything in my life. It's not like I want to get rid of him, you know."

"I know."

He just shakes his head again. Why isn't he fighting me? Questioning me? Maybe he agrees with me that I'm not doing a great job. Maybe he always knew, and never wanted to tell me.

"I just think... Now that I'm alone... I can't really take care of him... he needs more than I can give him."

Lupino nods.

"I cannot say I blame you, though I must admit it is hard for me to understand. We live dangerous lives, it is true. But... have you thought about what we spoke of, before your disappearance?"

I nod, again.

"Yeah, I have. But there's too many things I have to take care of, still. Things are too tense for me to leave."

"Alex... I will not force your hand, no matter what you decide. But please, think about this. This is your boy. You are his father. Please take a few weeks off. You have seen that the world will not end if you do. Will you not take some time to think on your decision?"

I sigh and nod. He looks at Nicolas, holding him in his arms. After a long moment, he hands him back to me, and clears his throat.

"I will be in contact with my lawyer. To make your decision, I believe you will need to know what your options are."

"Thank you, mister Lupino."

He stays quiet again for a while, staring at the floor, thinking. When he looks back up at me, his eyes are a bit wetter than I'd like, and his voice husky with grief.

"I think we will need to share a drink."

"I don't..."

"Yes. I know. You do not drink. I will give you something without alcohol. When men have a drink together, they do it for the company, not the effects. You are a stronger man than I, Alex. It takes a strong character, and a strong love, to be able to know that sometimes, loving someone means letting someone else take care of them."

He pats my cheek gently.

"I do not have that strength for you, though perhaps I should."

I frown, and I wonder what that means. Is he saying he would make me leave? I guess he doesn't understand. I'm not good with words, but maybe I can explain.

"You know, mister Lupino, we don't choose our parents, or I wouldn't have chosen mine. He can't choose me, and I can't give him a crappy life because of what I want. But the people I chose, I don't regret them. I certainly don't regret you."

He smiles at me, and nods once.

"Thank you, Alex. Now, let me get those drinks."

He stands, and walks to the kitchen. I look at Nicolas. I will think about it, like Lupino asked, but at the same time, I'm pretty sure of my decision. It's not just about the job, either. I know I could probably go flip burgers and be all right. But if people are going to come after me for being what I am, then there's no way I can keep him safe. And we might have taken down these guys; but Julie said they had other offices. It seems like only a matter of time before they, or someone else, comes after me again. I can't change what I am. But I can give him a chance. After all, as a father, I have to give him the best; and a chance is pretty much the only thing I have to give.

ACKNOWLEDGEMENTS

I hate acknowledgements.

Don't get me wrong, I find myself being grateful on a regular basis, but I don't say it as often as I should, because there doesn't seem to be any good way to do justice to the profound impact that people can have in my life, and my career as a writer.

First of all, as always, a huge thank you to those of you who read it first, and who helped give it birth. Jessica, Manon, Marie-Claude, Marjolaine, you are the best critique group anyone could ask for. I am grateful to have you in my life. Thank you for the corrections, thank you for the encouragements, thank you for driving me on, whether or not you realized you were doing it.

Also, in particular, I owe a huge debt of gratitude to Franck, who designed this cover and the one for *Blood Relations*. Thank you for your wonderful art, for taking the time to read the books, and your amazing friendship.

It seems appropriate that I should thank my family, whether by blood or by choice, since it's such an important theme of this book and series. So in that spirit, thank you to Phil, Joelle, Émilie, Manue, Annie, mom. Your encouragements, interest, and occasional hard truths keep me going.

A big thank you to my amazing colleagues from the Vanier and Rideau branches of the Ottawa Public Library.

Finally, as always, to Mathieu, my partner in all things, thank you for being my creative sounding board, and the person that weathers my dark moments.

Last, but certainly not least, to the extraordinary team at Renaissance Press, thank you for bringing this to life, and for pouring your hearts and souls into projects like these.

ABOUT THE AUTHOR

Caroline Fréchette is a sequential artist and author. She has published several short stories, both sequential and traditional, as well as two graphic novels, all on the French Canadian and European markets. She was the editor and director for the French Canadian literary magazine *Histoires à boire debout,* and works in a library. She has been teaching creative writing since 2005, and manages the writing page *Ice Cream for Zombies. Brothers In Arms* is book 2 in the *Family by Choice series.* For more information, you can visit her website at carolinefrechette.com.

PREVIEW - KINDRED SPIRITS

MAY 17TH, 5:57 PM

Julie stops the car in front of her office. I've only been here once or twice; it's in a small building in Old Town, so of course Jimmy's already here, smoking a cigarette, leaning on the wall by the door. He must have come straight from Erik's place, because he's still wearing that stupid The Clash t-shirt. He notices us and waves.

We all get out of the car. I see that Dow has gotten here too, and is waiting in his SUV. When he gets out of it to approach us, he eyes Jimmy suspiciously. He must have heard of him; there's very few people who know this town's underworld that haven't. We gather in front of the building, and Julie takes out her keys to unlock the door, peering through the window. Jimmy watches her, and nods at me.

"How come you're always getting in trouble?"

I shrug.

"Hey, when you can do what I can, you draw attention. You should know; you draw your fair share too, you know."

"Why'd you need me here, anyway? There's no one. I checked."

"Just in case."

He has a grin, and looks at my companions, then me.

"So, a bunch of superheroes need help from a guy like me, huh? I'm flattered."

I nudge him with my elbow.

"Don't let your head get too big."

"What, you mean, like, as big as yours?"

Julie rolls her eyes, and walks in.

"Settle down, boys. It doesn't look like we'll need you after all. Doesn't seem like anyone's been here."

We walk in after her, and she's right. The place is spotless. Well, it's dirty, but it's her kind of dirty, not like someone searched through it or anything. She goes to the desk and sits behind it, leaning down to retrieve something from under it. I relax and against the wall. Dow seems tense, looking around, but then he's not used to being in the situation we're in now, and, to me, he always seems tense. Tom, though, is fidgeting nervously, and he looks nauseous. He gets that way around Jimmy, but this time, it seems worse.

"You ok, Tom?"

He makes a face, and shrugs.

"I don't know. I don't feel so good."

"What do you mean? Is it something you ate?"

He shakes his head. He's still looking worried, and it's starting to make me nervous.

"No... it's not that kind of thing. It's more... like a feeling. A feeling that something bad is gonna happen."

I frown. He's never made predictions before, but coming from that kid, I'd be willing to believe he could turn into a badger.

"Something bad how?"

"I don't know, exactly... just... I have this weird feeling. And I feel kind of... fuzzy."

Suddenly, he looks right at my eyes, alarmed.

"I can't hear you."

This makes Julie look up sharply, frowning.

"What do you mean?"

His eyes are wide, and he turns to look out the window.

"I can't hear your thoughts."

She stands, putting something in her pocket.

"I got what we came for. Let's go. Now."

I nod, and as we turn to exit, the window suddenly shatters. I duck, pulling Tom down with me. I didn't hear anything. Jimmy crouches next to the window immediately, grabbing a gun out of his coat, looking at the street. Julie ducks behind her desk, as Dow stands around, fidgeting, apparently unsure of what to do.

"Get down, Dow!"

He stares at me for about a second, which is a second too much, because I hear something that sounds a bit like a muffled gunshot, and he goes down. I curse, and look at Tom.

"Do whatever you gotta do, but stay down, is that clear?"

He nods. I don't think I've ever seen him scared, and I've lived with him for almost a year now. Then again, he spent years at GenEx, and he's never seen a null strong enough to cancel out his power. I get up, not standing but crouching so I'm still under relative cover, and try to summon the fire. It doesn't come, of course. I half-crawl, half-walk to join Jimmy by the side of the window. He's not shooting, so I guess he hasn't found a target, and I look out. There doesn't seem to be anything out there. Nothing I can see, anyway. I turn around to look at my companions. Dow is still lying on the floor, but there's no blood. Julie's hiding behind her desk, and she seems furious. I look back at Jimmy.

"See anything?"

He shakes his head.

"Best check on your friend."

I turn to inspect Dow again. There's still no blood, so that's reassuring. And then, I notice it; there's a small red dart embedded in his upper arm.

"They're using tranquilizer guns!"

"I see something!"

I turn around. Jimmy's looking towards the door. I look, and see something moving, but it's way too fast. Suddenly the glass on the door shatters and something that looks like a tin can flies through it, rolling on the floor. I shout as I recognize what it is.

"Tear gas!"

Julie's moving towards Tom, who seems a little lost without his power, and I decide to go for Dow under the cover of the gas. I run, crouching, but there's another shot, and what hits my leg hurts way too much to be a tranquilizer dart. I scream and fall on my knees, and when I look, there's blood gushing from my thigh, and it hurts like hell. I've been shot before, in the gut, and I don't remember it hurting like that. The room is quickly filling with vapor, and soon the only person I can see is Jimmy. He's looking out the window, and finally seeing something, because he shoots his gun twice, before some guy comes running at him so fast he seems to appear out of nowhere, grabbing his gun hand and tackling him to the floor. I try to stand and help him, but when I lean on my leg, it feels like it's tearing open all over again, and I stumble. Before I can even think about trying again, a huge guy steps through the broken window and grabs me by the back of the collar, then hurls me across the room. I crash over Julie's desk, hitting my side, and by the angle and the pain, I can tell I've broken or at least cracked a couple of ribs, because I recognize the feeling.

I try to push myself up, which is impossibly painful because of the leg and the ribs, and my eyes are starting to burn. I wheeze, trying to refrain from coughing, because with everything else, the pain in my ribs might make me pass out. I can hear more than see the huge guy walking towards me, and I try to make the fire, but of course, my power still doesn't work, so I look frantically for anything on the desk I can use to defend myself. I hear more gunshots as my hand closes on a heavy metal three-hole punch. I can feel him right behind me, and before he grabs me again, I turn around, using the motion to put weight into the blow I strike, right to his head, with the three-hole punch. He stumbles back again, so, using the desk to lean on, I hit him again, and again. Every time hurts, but if he gets his hands on me one last time, with the state I'm in and no powers, I'm done for, so I put all my desperation in my arm. It won't be enough, I know, but if I'm going down, it sure as hell won't be without a fight. I move to hit him again, and he grabs my forearm, lifting me up by it, yanking the punch out of my hand. I have time to get the satisfaction of seeing his face mangled and bloody where I hit him before he throws me to the ground and starts wailing on me.

My mouth tastes like blood, and I'm about to pass out when suddenly, there's a loud popping sound, and a flash of light. It attracts the huge guy's attention, and he turns to look over his shoulder to see. I try to hit him again, but I somehow can hardly lift my arm. The smoke suddenly clears, and I can see a guy walking towards me. He looks weirdly familiar. It's as if I'm looking at Tom, but taller, leaner, meaner, and with a lot more scars. Then, he raises his hands, glaring at the giant, and the huge guy grabs his head and moans, and just falls, crushing me with his weight. The pain in my ribs is too much to bear, and I pass out.

www.ingramcontent.com/pod-product-compliance
Lightning Source LLC
Chambersburg PA
CBHW071312250626

47159CB00004B/1393